It Ain't All
For Nothin'

Also by Walter Dean Myers

Fiction

HANDBOOK FOR BOYS

MONSTER
Michael L. Printz Award
Coretta Scott King Author Honor Book
National Book Award Finalist

THE MOUSE RAP

THE RIGHTEOUS REVENGE OF ARTEMIS BONNER

SCORPIONS
A Newbery Honor Book

THE STORY OF THE THREE KINGDOMS

Nonfiction

ANGEL TO ANGEL: A Mother's Gift of Love

BAD BOY: A Memoir

BROWN ANGELS: An Album of Pictures and Verse

MALCOLM X: A Fire Burning Brightly

NOW IS YOUR TIME!: The African-American
Struggle for Freedom
Coretta Scott King Author Award

Awards

*ALA Margaret A. Edwards Award for lifetime
achievement in writing for young adults*
*ALAN Award for outstanding contribution to
the field of young adult literature*

GRANDMA CARRIE'S BEEN SICK

Two days later a doctor came by with the welfare lady. What they said was that Grandma Carrie couldn't take care of herself any more. She couldn't even do little things, and even though we started getting the checks from the welfare it didn't do much good because all we did was to eat and sleep and watch television or read from the Bible. I used to have to help Grandma Carrie to go to the bathroom, and it wasn't hard to do because she was getting smaller all the time. She was getting smaller until she begin to look like a old child, or maybe a sickly one. Then she couldn't even go to the bathroom at all, and I told that to Miss Hattie, and the welfare people came and talked to her and said that she had to go to a home for old people. The arthritis had made her knuckles and her knee joints swell up. That was how come I started living with Lonnie.

WALTER DEAN MYERS

It Ain't All For Nothin'

≋ HarperTrophy®

Amistad

Amistad is an imprint of HarperCollins Publishers.

Harper Trophy® is a registered trademark of
HarperCollins Publishers Inc.

Library of Congress Cataloging-in-Publication Data
Myers, Walter Dean.
    It ain't all for nothin' / Walter Dean Myers
        p.   cm.
    Summary: A young black boy must decide whether to
go along with his father, who is a thief, or reject his father's
way of life and risk losing him.
    ISBN 0-06-447311-2 (pbk.)
    [1. Fathers and sons—Fiction.]   I. Title.
PZ7.M992It   78-57516
[Fic]   CIP
                                                        AC

Typography by Karin Paprocki
❖
First Harper Trophy edition, 2003
Visit us on the World Wide Web!
www.harperteen.com
20 OPM 14

In memory of my brother
George Douglas Myers

It Ain't All For Nothin'

1

Grandma Carrie used to get money from Social Security, and sometimes she did day's work. Things had been going pretty much all right with us. Most of the day's work wasn't really working because she used to go up to the house of a lady she knew real well and they would drink coffee and talk about different things. The lady's name was Mrs. Lilly. I saw her sometimes on Sundays after we got out of church and me and Grandma Carrie would take the subway over to where she lived. She was old like Grandma Carrie, and she was a lot smaller, too. Grandma Carrie was almost as big as a man. She always said when she was young she didn't have time to be studying on being little and things like that—she had to get out and work. She was strong-looking, too. She said when you can't reach around and grab nothing to help you, and you didn't have a man to hold on to, you had to reach inside yourself and find something strong. I guess she must have done that because, like I said, we wasn't doing too bad.

Mrs. Lilly was Jewish and lived clear out in Brooklyn, away from where the black people lived. Me and Grandma Carrie lived on Manhattan Avenue near 125th Street. It used to take us a hour or more to get to Mrs. Lilly's place. She lived in a old building that smelled like it was a museum or something. She had a son somewhere who worked down on Wall Street, and he used to send her money once a week, and he would come to see her about twice a month. Mrs. Lilly told Grandma Carrie that she would like to see him more, but she knew he had a family of his own and everything. She said sometimes she spent all day thinking about if she should call him or not, then when she did call him she wouldn't even know what to say. She said he was a good son and he wanted her to come and live with him, but she wouldn't do it because she didn't want to be a burden.

Then one day Mrs. Lilly told Grandma Carrie that her son was sending her to Florida.

"You got people in Florida?" Grandma Carrie asked.

Mrs. Lilly said that she didn't but that her son thought it was a good idea. They both talked about her going to Florida like it was a good thing, but when the time come for her to go she was crying and so was Grandma Carrie. When Mrs. Lilly was getting into the car, she told Grandma Carrie that she didn't think she was going to live a long time. Her son was saying things to try to make her stop crying, but she didn't. Then they was gone off in the car, and me and Grandma Carrie was standing there with a suitcase and two shopping bags full of stuff that Mrs. Lilly had give to us. We took the stuff on home, and I could see that Grandma Carrie had something on her mind. She was real quiet and sat on the edge of the bed and rocked a little. I asked her what it was that was wrong, but she didn't say nothing. I wanted to go out and see what was going on outside, but when Grandma Carrie got into one of her rocking moods it wasn't much good to ask her to go out. I looked at the paper for a while in the kitchen, and then I heard her speak out. I didn't hear what she said, so I went into the bedroom and she said it again.

"You know she gave us a nice piece of money every week," Grandma said. "I don't know what we gonna do now, boy. Guess the Lord will provide."

She didn't say much more about it then, and I didn't ask her nothing, either. We watched television for a while, and then she called me in for Sunday evening prayer.

"Lord, this is Your servant Carrie. Thank You, Jesus, for looking out after me and this boy today. Thank You, Jesus, for providing us with the meals to nourish our earthly bodies. Thank You, Jesus, for providing us with Your love to nourish our heavenly spirits.

"Lord, take care of Mrs. Lilly so that she can seek Thy grace and the peace of Thy love. Go ahead, boy."

"Thank You, Jesus, for our daily bread. Thank You, Jesus, for the love You have shown us and for Your mercy. Amen."

"You thanking Jesus from your heart or you thanking Him from memory, boy?"

"I'm thanking Him from my heart, Grandma Carrie."

"Go on to bed."

I went on to bed, and things went on about like they used to except for Grandma Carrie not going to see Mrs. Lilly. Grandma Carrie said we had to cut back on spending, and I said okay. It was summertime and school was out, so I didn't have much to spend on, anyway. Grandma Carrie said we was poor in the ways of the world but rich in the spirit of Jesus. That was okay with me, because we always had enough to eat and everything, anyway. Sometimes I would go down to the market and either carry bags for people or help them clean out the vegetable department. The man who was the manager of the produce department was named Sal, and he didn't work you too hard, and he always gave you fifty cents or a dollar extra if you didn't fool around.

Grandma said that she had to go out and get a job because I was looking raggedy. I did need new sneakers, but I really wasn't looking raggedy. That was just the way Grandma Carrie talked all the time. If you was a little dirty she would say that you must be getting ready to plant potatoes because you got so much dirt stored away. That's the kind of thing she would say. She went downtown and got a job from the State, and she went out to work the next day. When she come home I had made supper. I had cooked some collards with a streak of lean in them and made some rice. I cut up the pork butt she had made on Sunday and put it in with the collards when they was almost done. Grandma Carrie said that she wasn't hungry. I looked at her and I knew she wasn't feeling too good. She wasn't ailing or anything like that—she just looked like she was drooping over. When she was praying that night I could hear her asking for strength to make another day.

"Let me make another day, Jesus, just one more.

I know You tired of carrying my burden, but there ain't but a few steps more. . . ."

I never really liked it when she got to praying too hard because I knew she was sad. I listened real hard to hear if she called my mother's name and she did. Sometimes she would pray things about my mother, about things they used to do together before my mother got married, and I would listen to her.

"Jesus, You remember that time when Esther won that prize in school for being the prettiest child? And how we walked all around the school-yard afterwards and she was just beaming, Jesus? You know she was just beaming, Jesus."

I liked to hear Grandma Carrie talk about my mother. I didn't like it when she was sad, which was the only time she mostly prayed about my mother, but I liked hearing about her. She would never talk about her when she wasn't sad or wasn't praying. Sometimes she would pray about how I was born, which was when my mother died. She died having me, so I never got to know her. When I would ask Grandma Carrie to talk about her when she wasn't praying, she would say there wasn't no use in studying on the dead.

"Hard as life is, what you want to go and study on dyin' for?" she would say. But she would hug me, and sometimes she would get to rocking and crying a little, not out loud, but you could see her eyes filling up, and I know she was thinking about my mother. She always talked about her as "that girl," and sometimes I used to imagine her as being a little girl that I could play with.

Jesus gave Grandma Carrie strength for another day, but it got harder and harder for her. When she had been doing day's work for Mrs. Lilly, they would do the dusting and things together and it wasn't too hard. Now soon's she came home she was ready to go to bed. And sometimes if she prayed too long she would have to call me in and get me to help her off her knees. Then one day I was in the park playing stickball with Earl and Little Mike and some other guys when Shirley Glover came up and said that Grandma Carrie had fallen down in the hallway.

"She still there?" I asked.

"No, stupid, a man helped her up," Shirley said, "but I think she hurt her hip or her back or something."

I went on home and found Grandma Carrie making supper. She looked okay and I asked her how she felt.

"Feel like I'm sixty-nine years old, which I am," she said, sprinkling some flour from the sifter over the onions in the pan. "And I also feel like I don't have to be reporting to no tadpole how I feel all the time."

"Shirley said you fell down in the hallway."

"Shirley Glover?"

"Yes, ma'am."

"Anybody can fall down," she said. "Won't be the last time, Lord knows. You wash your hands and get ready for supper. You change that shirt from yesterday?"

"I think so," I called back as I went into the bathroom.

"The stink don't think so!"

I had meant to change the shirt, but I forgot because I had been in a hurry. I took it off and smelled under the arms and it didn't really smell that bad, even though it didn't smell so good, either. I looked in the hamper and there was another shirt in there that wasn't wrinkled too bad and didn't smell too bad, so I put that one on and put the smelly one in the hamper. When I finished washing I went into the kitchen and Grandma Carrie was leaning against the refrigerator holding her side. I asked her what was wrong and she just shook her head the way she did when she was hurting too bad to be talking about it. She had already put my plate out and I sat down and said grace and started eating.

"Get up and help me into the room, boy."

I moved the chair out of the way first and then I put my arm around her and stood so she could lean on me. Every time she took a step, even a little step with her left leg, which was on the same side that she was holding, her face twisted up. I had just about caught up with her in size, but she was bent over now and I could feel her breathing on my face. Every time she took a step she would let out two or three little breaths. She wanted to sit down for a while, but I told her she might as well lay down on the bed, and she said okay.

We got to the bed and she couldn't even lay down without me giving her a hand.

"You want me to fix you a plate and bring it in?" I asked.

"Just make me some peppermint tea," she said. When she lay back on the pillows a little sharp sound come out of her, and I know she was hurting pretty bad.

I put the water on and got a cup down to make the tea. There was a roach in the cup and I nearly dropped it. I was glad that I didn't because it was one of the big cups that she liked so much. It had blue decorations on it and birds and some other things that looked Japanesy. I rinsed out the cup and sat down and waited for the water to boil. I saw the roach again—I had just shook him out of the cup and now he was crawling around on the shelf under the cupboard. I took a piece of cardboard and brushed it on the floor so I could step on him, but then I saw that he was bigger than I thought he was. I don't like to step on roaches if they're too big because they make a noise. Grandma Carrie said that they don't, but I think they do.

I made the tea and took it in to her, and she was so quiet I thought she was asleep.

"Grandma Carrie?"

"Put the tea down."

I put it down and went and got my plate and finished eating in the bedroom. She told me to get her some aspirins, and I did that, and she took two of them. From her bedroom you could only see the television at a angle, and so I turned it around and we watched some programs until she fell asleep, and then I went in the living room and turned on the baseball game. She would never watch the baseball games because she said there was colored on all the teams now, and so it didn't matter who won. Not since Jackie stopped playing, anyway.

Later I woke her up so she could take her clothes off and go to bed, and she had me to help her into the bathroom. I asked her if she wanted me to call for a doctor or anything, and she said no, she didn't want that. So I helped her to the bathroom and then back to the bed.

In the morning when I got up she was awake and sitting up on the bed, but she had the same clothes on from the night before. She told me to go and call Miss Hattie, a friend of hers, and I did that. Miss Hattie came over right away when I told her that Grandma Carrie wasn't feeling good. Grandma Carrie asked Miss Hattie to wait for the mailman and get her Social Security check and bring it to her so she could sign it, and then she was going to call for the doctor. Miss Hattie made some tea for Grandma Carrie and sent me to her house to get the pot of coffee that was still warm on the stove. They sat down and had their tea and coffee and talked. I waited downstairs for the mailman, and when I saw him coming I came up and told Miss Hattie, and she took the key and went, and sure enough, the check did come on time. Grandma Carrie signed it and Miss Hattie took it to the liquor store and cashed it with her cousin, who worked there. She brought the money back, and Grandma Carrie put it in her bosom, and then Miss Hattie called from her house to get a ambulance.

The ambulance didn't even come until that afternoon, and Miss Hattie asked the driver what took him so long.

"It's simple, lady," he said. "We got more people calling for ambulances than we got ambulances."

"Only thing that's simple is you, you simple fool!" When Miss Hattie got mad her eyes popped out and she would start blinking a lot.

They carried Grandma Carrie down the stairs on a stretcher, with me and Miss Hattie going down behind her and Miss Hattie saying things to Grandma Carrie to make her feel good. She said that she shouldn't be worried none or anything like that because she'd be up on her feet in no time. Downstairs a lot of the guys was standing around to see who it was they was taking to the hospital. The guys who rode in the back of the ambulance with Grandma Carrie said that I couldn't go in the ambulance, but I could go to the hospital on my own if I wanted to.

I ran down the block as fast as I could so I would get to the hospital about the same time as the ambulance, but it passed me up in the next block. I still ran for a little bit, but then I had to slow down because I got a stitch in my side. I got to the hospital after a while and asked a nurse if she had seen Grandma Carrie and she asked what her last name was and I said Brown. Her name was Carrie Brown, and the nurse said that she wasn't in that hospital as far as she knew. I thought I had went to the wrong hospital and was just about ready to run over to Metropolitan, which was down from Mount Morris Park, when I saw one of the guys who had picked up Grandma Carrie in the ambulance. I went over to him and asked him where she was, and he told me to go down the hall and make a left and she was on one of the rollers.

I didn't know what a roller was, but I did like he told me to and went down the hall and made a left, and there was Grandma Carrie on one of those things they push around the hospital.

"Grandma Carrie."

"Tippy?" She opened her eyes, and when she saw me she smiled some, and I smiled because I was glad to see her smiling. "How you get here so soon—you fly or something?"

"How come they got you out here in the hall-way?" I asked.

"They waitin' until a doctor is free," she said. "How you doing?"

"Okay."

"You ain't worried about me, are you?" she asked.

"I don't know." She seemed littler than she did most of the time, and she was kind of gray instead of being brown. Mostly, when she was okay and everything, she was brown like giblet gravy.

"Well, ain't no use in you being worried none." She reached out and put her hand on my shoulder and then down my arm, and I took her hand and held it in mine. "Ain't nothing wrong with me except old age, you know. The parts is just wearing down."

I didn't say nothing and she didn't say nothing, and so we just stayed there for a while waiting. A guy was mopping down the hall with ammonia and I thought it was going to upset her 'cause she really can't stand the smell of ammonia, but it didn't. I watched the guy pull the big mop over the floor. Every time he swung the mop there would be a little path of bubbles behind it, but they wouldn't last. He mopped right around us like we wasn't even there. He didn't look at us either, and I thought that maybe he went around all the time not seeing people or hearing things. Maybe he just didn't like mopping.

After a while a doctor came and looked at Grandma Carrie. He asked her some questions about how she felt and all and did she ever have trouble with her heart. Then he listen to her heart and told her to take some deep breaths. She did them all okay, and then he looked at her ankles and asked her if she ever had diabetes, and she said no. He kind of nodded like he knew something and wrote on a board he carried around. Then the doctor left and a nurse came and started pushing Grandma Carrie into a room with some other people.

"She got to stay in the hospital?" I asked. The nurse was sliding Grandma Carrie into a regular bed.

"Yeah." The nurse looked over at me and then leaned back to get a good look. "How old are you?"

"Twelve."

"Twelve? You ain't even supposed to be in here. Now why don't you go on out to the waiting area where you belong 'fore you gets me in trouble."

"I got to tell him what to do 'cause he don't know." Grandma Carrie rose up on one elbow and reached out for me, and I couldn't even hardly see her 'cause I was fixing to cry so bad. "We live alone, so I got to tell him what to do."

"You just lay yourself on down, woman," the nurse said. "He ain't supposed to be here, and when I get back in fifteen minutes he'd better be gone, too."

Then the nurse left, and I went up to Grandma Carrie, and she wiped my face with her hands, but I couldn't stop crying, no matter how hard I was wanting to.

"What you crying for?" she said. "Every strick of fat don't have a strick of lean. You old enough to know that, ain't you?"

"Yes, ma'am."

"And you got Jesus in your heart, ain't you?"

"Yes, ma'am."

"Then you ain't got not a thing to worry about, so just suck up them titty tears and hold your head up. You hear me?"

I nodded that I did and tried to hold back the crying best I could.

"Now you go on home and get the money from under my pillow. You take that money on down to Key Food and buy some groceries. Don't be buying no foolishness, either. I don't want to come home and see none of that crispy sugar mess. You buy some real food. Spend half the money on food and the other half you put in some place safe. Don't tell nobody you got it, either. Then tomorrow you go over to where your daddy stays and tell him to come up here. You get them groceries first, you hear?"

"Yes, ma'am."

"Now go on out of here, and if anybody asks you anything just tell them I'm going to be staying here for a day or two. And don't you forget to thank Jesus tonight."

I went out to the front of the hospital, where they had chairs for people to wait on, and into the bathroom. When I came out of the bathroom I saw everybody just sitting around and I sat with them. I knew Grandma Carrie had said for me to go straight out and buy the food, but I didn't want to leave the hospital. I looked at some magazines they had laying around and sometimes I looked at the other people. I had my keys around my neck on a chain I had got about a year ago, so I knew I could get into the house, but it didn't seem like a place to go without Grandma Carrie being there or me waiting for her to come. I didn't want to feel sad or anything, but I did, and after a while, when I had looked at the magazine over and over and the clock didn't even hardly move, I just got up and left.

It was a nice day, the kind of day you think everything is going to be all right on. But when I got down to 127th Street I saw a dead pigeon laying in the street. One of the things I can't stand to see is a dead pigeon, and the other is a dead dog or cat. Pigeons are the worse, though. Sometimes when you see pigeons laying in the street, the feathers on their chests looks purple. I don't want to look at it but I almost have to. When I saw this pigeon, dead and scrunched up against the curb, I crossed the street.

"What's the matter with your grandma?" Mrs. Glover was sitting out in front on the stoop with Shirley and Mrs. Bellinger.

"She's sick," I said.

"I know that!" Mrs. Glover said. "I asked what was wrong with her."

"I don't know." I was already going past them as I answered.

"Don't get fresh with me!" Mrs. Glover had the loudest voice of anyone I knew. Grandma Carrie said that Mrs. Glover never liked her because she wouldn't let her get into her business. I kept on going in the hallway, and I could hear Mrs. Glover still yelling at me, and then I heard somebody running behind me. I turned and it was Shirley.

"She was just asking to be polite!" Shirley said, getting real close to me and looking like she was real mad. I looked back at her the same way and even worse. "Just because you're so smart your grandmother's gonna die. You just wait and see."

Then she made another face and went back out on the stoop with her mother. I went on upstairs wondering if she was right. If God would get

Grandma Carrie because of something I said. It bothered me some, but then I just pushed it right out of my mind. I ate some leftover chicken stew and waited until it got to be nighttime, and then I watched television until it was time to go to bed.

I couldn't sleep because I kept thinking I heard noises in Grandma Carrie's room. I put the television on, which was good. I couldn't hear any noises and if Grandma Carrie did come home she would turn it off. Then I went to sleep.

I woke up early. I can usually tell what time it is by how the sun comes along the floor in the morning. Once I even marked off the different times on the linoleum. There was a flower—it was blue with red around the edges—and when the sun reached that flower, when it just barely touched it, it was seven o'clock. When I woke up, the first thing I did was to look on the floor, and the sun was about half a sneaker away from the flower, so I knew it was early. The next thing I did was go to Grandma Carrie's room just in case the whole thing was a bad dream. The bed was empty. It wasn't no dream. I felt bad and then I told myself to go on and do like she told me. I got dressed, took the money from under the pillow, and went out and bought some food, mostly soup and some boxes of frozen vegetables. I also bought some hamburger meat. I took everything upstairs and then started over to St. Nicholas Avenue where Lonnie stayed.

Lonnie is my father. What happened was that he and my mother got married and then, when my mother was having me, she died. That's what Grandma Carrie said. After she died Grandma Carrie said that she didn't want to have nothing to do with either me or Lonnie because she thought that we was the ones that made Esther die. She said that when she come home from the funeral she didn't even think about me—she just prayed very hard that everything would be all right for Esther when she got to heaven.

Then one day, while she was praying, she said something come over her and she felt that she just had to go over to where Lonnie was staying to see me. She came over to where we was, and she said I was real dirty and not looking very good and that Lonnie was watching television. She had asked Lonnie how come he didn't take care of me, and he said that he didn't know nothing about taking care of no babies, so then she took me. She had me ever since. When I was small Lonnie used to come around and see me sometimes, but then he stopped coming. I had asked Grandma Carrie why he stopped, and she said that he had to go away for a while. He came around to see me when he got back, but just once in a while, and then he would try to borrow money from Grandma Carrie but she wouldn't give him none.

I don't look much like Lonnie, but I wish I did 'cause I like the way he look. Sometimes I think about growing up and looking like him. Grandma Carrie said I was the spitting image of my mother, though, and that one day, when she could bear to see them again, she would take out some pictures of her and show them to me and I could see for myself.

For a while I forgot which house he lived in, but then I remembered that it was 427. It was a brownstone house, and I went up the front steps to ring the bell, but there wasn't any bell, just two wires sticking out and they was all taped up. I knew he lived on the second floor, in the back, and the door was open, so I just walked in.

It wasn't a nice place. Once when he took me to his house there was a guy who had been cut sitting on the floor in the hallway, and we just stepped around him and went on upstairs. It always smelled like somebody peed in the hallway, and you had to hold your breath when you went upstairs. On the second floor the smell wasn't so bad, but there was a bag of garbage on the floor and half of it was out. I knocked on Lonnie's door.

At first there was no answer and so I knocked again, and I was just figuring that nobody was home when the door opened a little and he peeked out and saw me.

"What you doing here?" he said.

"Grandma Carrie told me to come," I said.

"What she want now?" He opened the door and he only had his underpants on. He looked mad and I thought I should have waited until later to wake him up. He had also grown a little beard.

"She's in the hospital and she said she wants you to come over and see her," I said.

"What's the matter, she sick?"

"Uh-huh. She went to the hospital yesterday in a ambulance."

"What hospital she be in?" he said, moving away from in front of the door. "Come on in."

There was a lady sleeping on the bed. She was about as dark as me. There was some empty glasses on the bureau and a loaf of bread. Lonnie put on his pants and then he put some water in a pot and put it on, I guessed, for coffee or tea. The lady on the bed moved around even though she was still sleeping.

"What hospital you say she in?"

"She's in Knickerbocker," I said. "She told me to come up here and tell you to come over."

"Where you staying now?"

"Home."

"She say what she want to see me for?"

"No. I guess because she sick."

"I ain't no damn doctor!"

I didn't say nothing because he looked mad again. He went on into the bathroom, and I could hear him using the toilet through the door and I just stood there. The lady on the bed woke up and she looked over at me and then looked around the room.

"Where's Lonnie?"

"In the bathroom."

"Who you?"

"Tippy," I said, just as Lonnie was coming out of the bathroom. Lonnie made some instant coffee. He drank down half of it and then gave the other half to the lady and she started sipping on it.

"You see Carrie, you tell her I'll check her out later," he said. He was holding up a shirt to see if he wanted to wear it.

"You're not coming now?" I asked.

He didn't say nothing. He just put the shirt down and turned and looked at me like I had really done something wrong. Then he went and opened the door. He just stood there with it open, and then I went out.

"I'll see you later," I said. But he just closed the door.

I thought about going back to the hospital and telling Grandma Carrie that Lonnie wouldn't come. Then I started trying to remember if she had said that he should come right away or just come. I couldn't remember so I just went home. I looked to see where the money was and it was still where I put it. There was some dirty dishes in the sink and I washed them. I thought about fixing something to eat but I wasn't really hungry so I didn't. I thought about laying down and I wasn't tired, and I thought about watching some television but there wasn't anything on I wanted to see. So I just hung around for the rest of the evening and waited for the next day. While I was waiting around I thought about Lonnie not going to the hospital. I didn't think he liked Grandma Carrie much. He didn't like me too much, either.

Grandma Carrie stayed in the hospital for three more days before she came out. She looked like she lost most of the front of her. If you looked at her from the back she looked all right, but from the front she looked like she was hollowed out. She was supposed to go back to the hospital clinic every Tuesday for treatment, but sometimes she didn't go. When it rained a lot or was fixing to rain she took a lot of aspirins for the pain. She said she always had arthritis but now it was getting to be too bad. She could hardly walk around.

When we ran out of food money and the check from the Social Security didn't come on time, she got Miss Hattie to call welfare. I wished she didn't do that because I didn't want to be on welfare. A lot of people was on welfare, and it was all right around the block where we was, but if you talked about it in school you had to talk about it like it was a shameful thing. I didn't know if it was a shameful thing but I knew I didn't want to be on it. Mostly they was saying things in school about having babies without being married or having your father run away from you. Grandma Carrie wasn't having babies or anything like that. I didn't know if Lonnie had run away or not, because I knew just where he lived.

Miss Hattie said that the welfare people said that she had to go down there and talk to them, but Grandma Carrie asked Miss Hattie how she gonna go down there without no money.

"Ain't that the truth," Miss Hattie said. Miss Hattie was not as old as Grandma Carrie but she dressed older. She used to wear big hats and old-time dresses and those shoes with the fat heels on them. "Only way you can get some money from those people is when you got enough money to run around after them!"

A lady that lived on the third floor told Miss Hattie to call the police and they would get the welfare people to come see what the matter was. Miss Hattie did that and two policemen came around that afternoon.

"We got a report that there was a child being abused here," one of the policemen said. The other policeman sat down and took off his shoe and looked at his sock which had a small hole in it. Both of the policemen was black, but one looked kind of Spanish, too.

Grandma Carrie said that there wasn't no child being abused, only that we needed some money to live on, and they said okay, they would see what they could do about it. The one who did the most talking called Grandma Carrie "sister" all the time. When they left, Miss Hattie came back with some groceries she had bought for us, and Grandma Carrie thanked her and told me to thank her.

"Thank you, Miss Hattie." I was just about fixing to cry again because I didn't want to thank her. It made me feel real bad when she had to give us food to eat. I wished that I could have paid her some money for it but I didn't have any. I thought maybe I would go to the supermarket and get a part-time job or something.

Two welfare people and another policeman came to the house the next day. They were all white. They said that the police department reported a case of child abuse. They asked me when was it the last time I had something to eat. I told them that I ate every day. The woman asked Grandma Carrie a lot of questions, and the man asked me a lot of questions like where I went to school and whatnot. Then he told me to take my clothes off and he looked at me to see if I had any beat marks on me, which I didn't. Grandma Carrie was real strict but she was not the kind of person who was beating on you all the time. Afterwards they left me and they told Grandma Carrie what she would have to do and all.

They said that Lonnie would have to bring me down to the Department of Welfare and that she had to come down and fill out some papers for herself if she wanted to be on welfare. She said that she didn't have no money to come down in a taxi and she couldn't walk good enough to take no subway.

"I got to lay up here and die before you takes notice that I need something?" Grandma Carrie said. Her voice was not too strong, like a radio that you had to tune in better. "I've been a working woman all my life—I ain't asking for nothing 'cause I don't want to work."

She started crying, and it was the first time I seen her cry like that. She was crying deep from her chest, and tears was running down her face. Nobody said nothing. The white woman from the welfare department looked around for something and held her hands up to her chest like she didn't know what to do, and I thought that maybe she was gonna cry, too. The policeman walked in the other room with the man from welfare who had looked at me.

"Don't cry, Grandma Carrie." I tried to hold her hand, but she just kept on.

"You come back in here!" she called out to the policeman and the man from welfare.

"Please, Mrs. Brown, don't get yourself upset." The woman from the welfare came over and put her arm around Grandma Carrie, but Grandma Carrie pushed herself up on one elbow and called to the men again.

"You come back in here, I want to show you something!" she called out, and her voice was crying as she was talking.

They came back in and stood near the foot of the bed. The man from welfare looked down at the papers he had been filling out, and the policeman looked over at the woman who had her arm around Grandma Carrie.

"Don't be looking down at them papers!" Grandma Carrie said. "You look up here at me. 'Cause I'm just what you gonna be one day—I'm old. And if you don't like it, it don't make no difference because that's what you all gonna be. So don't turn your back on me, just don't do it. . . ."

She was saying some other things, but you couldn't make out what they was because she was crying so bad. And the woman put her other arm around her and held her, and I just sort of stood, not knowing what to do or even what to say.

Two days later a doctor came by with the welfare lady. What they said was that Grandma Carrie couldn't take care of herself any more. She couldn't even do little things, and even though we started getting the checks from the welfare it didn't do much good because all we did was to eat and sleep and watch television or read from the Bible. I used to have to help Grandma Carrie to go to the bathroom, and it wasn't hard to do because she was getting smaller all the time. She was getting smaller until she begin to look like a old child, or maybe a sickly one. Then she couldn't even go to the bathroom at all, and I told that to Miss Hattie, and the welfare people came and talked to her and said that she had to go to a home for old people. The arthritis had made her knuckles and her knee joints swell up. That was how come I started living with Lonnie.

Lonnie had an apartment on St. Nicholas Avenue.
It was a old building and I didn't like it. It had two
rooms, a big one when you came in the door from
the outside and a small one that wasn't much bigger than Grandma Carrie's bathroom. There was a
cot in the small room plus a lot of boxes and things
that Lonnie used to keep his stuff in. He said that
he used to buy old stuff from people and keep it
until he could sell it for a good price. When I got
there, he took the boxes and things off the cot and
piled them in a corner. He told me I could keep
my things in the bottom drawer of the bureau. I
said okay.

There was a lot of things different living with
Lonnie than there was with Grandma Carrie. The
first thing was that Lonnie didn't do things at a set
time. He got up in the morning any time he wanted
to and went to bed any time he wanted to, too. He
never ate in the house at all. He used to go out and
eat. Sometimes he would eat at a friend's house and

sometimes he would just buy a frankfurter or something. It was all right living like that, I guess, but you never knew what to do. He had a little refrigerator—it wasn't as big as Grandma Carrie's—but he never kept no food in it. He wasn't easy to talk to, either. You could talk to Grandma Carrie about just anything. If you saw something on television and you said, "What you think about that?" she would say this or that or whatever she felt about it. But Lonnie wouldn't. If you asked him a question he'd always ask you a question. If you'd say, "What you think about that?" he'd say, "What did you think about it?"

Sometimes he wouldn't even answer your questions at all. He wouldn't give you a hard time but he didn't say nothing, like he didn't hear the question, and I thought maybe he was hard of hearing. But when Bubba or Stone came around he talked to them a lot. Bubba and Stone was two of Lonnie's friends. Sometimes they would come around and drink or they would play cards. I didn't like either of them. They didn't do nothing wrong, they just didn't look very nice. They always say you shouldn't judge people by how they look. But I always judge people by how they look. Usually if you find somebody who looks tough they are tough, and whatever you do they are gonna be tough, and if you're not tough they're gonna be tough on you. If you find somebody that don't look tough they may be tough but they don't pick on you. Bubba and Stone looked like I wouldn't like them. They cursed a lot, too. Every sentence they would say had at least one curse word in it. It was kind of funny because I remember Mr. Siegfried, the English teacher, saying that every sentence got to have a verb in it. Bubba and Stone must have went to a different school.

Sal didn't have no work, and I couldn't make much carrying packages, so I had to ask Lonnie for money to get something to eat. He said don't be coming to him all the time for money because he didn't have none, and I asked him if he was gonna buy some food, but he just got mad and didn't say anything. Later, when Bubba came up, he bought some doughnuts and Lonnie gave me two. He was telling Bubba that all I did was to sit around and grease. I didn't even want to eat the doughnuts, and I went on into my room and laid across the cot.

"Why don't you get on welfare?" I heard Bubba saying. "You can get welfare for him. My man Jackie, that cat that used to play ball up at City, used to get welfare when his old lady left him."

"He was on welfare when his grandmother had

him," Lonnie said.

"Hey, man, then you got it made," Bubba said. "Once he was on it once, they got to let him back on, man. They probably never took him off."

The next day me and Lonnie went down to the welfare office. He told me to go along with everything he said. That way we could get on, he said.

The big welfare office is a terrible place. There's all these benches you sit on and you have to wait until they call your name. Then you go up and tell them your story. The waiting around is the hard part. We got there at nine o'clock and the whole place was filled up. Some people was calling out things from the benches at the people who was working at the desks. There was a whole lot of children there, and some of them was running around, and some of them was crying. A woman with a baby was sitting next to where me, Lonnie, and Bubba was sitting. Bubba was telling Lonnie things to say, and then Lonnie was telling me. He told Lonnie to have me call him Daddy, instead of Lonnie.

"You hear that?" Lonnie asked.

"Yes," I said.

"Yes what?"

"Yes, I heard it."

"Man, what kind of punk lame is you, anyway?" Lonnie hit me in the chest with his elbow, and I wanted to just get up and run away. "Didn't you hear Bubba say you was supposed to call me Daddy?"

"Yes, Daddy."

I had always wanted to call him Daddy. I used to hear my friend Earl call his father Daddy, and I used to think about calling Lonnie that. But when he came over once and I called him Daddy he got real mad and said his name was Lonnie, it wasn't no damn Daddy. He made me feel ashamed to call him Daddy, and I still felt funny about it.

We just sat there, with Lonnie—I mean Daddy—talking with Bubba. A lot of people was talking about how bad the welfare people was. One woman said she didn't have nothing to eat in three days. She looked like she had been drinking. The more she talked the louder she got. The woman next to me with the baby smiled at me and offered me a piece of her candy bar. She wasn't so old, I know, because when I was in the fourth grade I used to see her going to Intermediate School. She got called in a little while, but when she came back she was crying, and I guess she didn't get what she wanted.

The woman who was getting very loud took off her hair. It wasn't her hair, it was a wig and underneath was her regular hair, and she had a pick and picked it out so it was kind of neat, but it still didn't look too good. The wig didn't look too good, either. All the time she was picking out her hair she kept saying that she was tired of these people messing over her.

"I might have to kill me somebody in here today!" she yelled at one of the guards. "Don't be looking at me with your liver-lipped self!" Everybody started turning around and looking at her, and she started yelling louder and louder, and finally the guard came over and got her name and they called her right away. When she got into the place where the desks were she was sitting near a pole and I couldn't see her too good, only her legs and her head when she leaned forward. But I could hear her, and she kept screaming and going on. Then she started swinging her arms around, and the lady who was talking to her got scared and stood up and told her to have a seat in the waiting area. She said she wasn't going no place until she got some help. Then the welfare people talked together for a while and sent her to get a check.

It was nearly two o'clock when me and Lonnie got called. He told the lady I was already on welfare, and they looked up my record. They asked him if he had a job, and he said no, he couldn't find no work and we was both hungry and he didn't know how he was going to pay his rent so we both might have to stay at the welfare shelter. The lady he was talking to gave him some papers to fill out, and he said he couldn't fill them out because he couldn't read or write. That was what Bubba had told him to say—that he couldn't read or write. The lady asked him if he had friends who could read or write, and he said no, and the lady got a very disgusted look on her face and started filling out the papers for him. When all the papers had been filled out, she told Lonnie that I would be put back on welfare but that his application would have to be processed. Then we left, and he told Bubba.

"I knew you would get over, man," Bubba said. "They can't mess with a kid, especially once they been on the sucker."

Lonnie said I didn't have to call him Daddy no more.

They had put Grandma Carrie back in the hospital, and I asked her what was wrong with her when I went to see her. She said there wasn't nothing wrong with her, just that she was old, like she said before. I saw she still couldn't get around good—her hands was really swoll up, and she was keeping one leg straight out. I didn't ask her why she kept that leg straight out like that. Sometimes when things happen bad to people I just don't want to know too much about it. I asked her was they giving her medicine and stuff and she said no, they just keeping her there because she was old.

She asked me how I was getting along and I said just fine.

"You saying your prayers every night?" she said. She was looking me straight in the face to see if I was gonna lie or anything.

"Not every night."

"Sometimes it ain't easy praying every night," she said. "Sometimes you think Jesus ain't listening, but He's listening. Jesus hears prayers, and that's the truth!"

We talked for a while longer. Some of the other people who was sitting downstairs in the hospital said hello to me, and she said that I was her grandson. They said I looked like a fine boy. Then we started running out of things to say to each other. When we was home we never ran out of things to say to each other because we knew everything about where we was and we could always talk on it if we wanted to. I didn't want to say good-bye because I felt sad for her. I thought about asking her if she was happy but I didn't.

When I got home the first check from the welfare had come, and Lonnie and Bubba had bought some groceries, and they was all happy about the money. Lonnie said he was gonna go downtown and buy him a coat and maybe he would buy me one, too. He said he was gonna buy one of those rabbit coats. They was so excited and talking so fast that it got me excited, too. Later on some girls came up. One girl by the name of Denise and another girl by the name of Lois. Lonnie gave me five dollars and told me to go to the movies. I thought they was going to fool around with those two girls. I didn't really care much, though.

I went around to the church, and Leon and

Randolph was both there. They was brothers and they wanted to be engineers when they grew up. I didn't know what I wanted to be when I grew up, even though sometimes I said I wanted to be a doctor or a guy who works making furniture. I was good in shop, and the teacher said I had good hands and a good feel for wood. Leon didn't have nothing to do and Randolph had to go help his mother do something, so I asked Leon if he wanted to go to the movies. He didn't have no money so I was going to help him pay his way, but his mother said he couldn't go anyway. I went by myself and saw a space picture by the name of *Star Wars*. I liked it a lot.

When I got home Lonnie wasn't there. I made a ham-and-cheese sandwich and washed up the dishes they had left behind. The room smelled funny, like somebody had been smoking herb, and I thought maybe it was Lonnie and them. I guess it had to be, but I was sorry that Lonnie did that if he did. Grandma Carrie always said that herb was just another thing to keep black people from doing what they was supposed to be doing.

It got late and I went to sleep.

The next day when I woke up Lonnie was already up and drinking coffee. He drank about as much coffee as Grandma Carrie did tea. He showed me a coat he had bought. It was leather and he had bought some shirts for me. There was one white one and two colored ones. He said he had to go downtown and take care of business, and he gave me five dollars more. I told him that I still had a dollar from the day before, and he said not to worry about it.

When I was living with Grandma Carrie she had shown me the welfare check. It was for ninety-four dollars. She said it was plenty for us to make it along with her Social Security. I figured that Lonnie must have got ninety-four dollars, too. I looked to see how much food he had bought, and it wasn't too much, so I put the five dollars in my room in a pair of rolled up socks in case he ran out of money. Then I took some Twinkies he had bought and went down to the stoop.

I liked sitting on the stoop a lot. It was real hot and most of the people on the block had different colored clothes on. In the wintertime most of the people wore brown clothes or dark-blue clothes. But in the summer they put on yellow and red and light-green clothes, and it was nice just to sit and look at them. By the time I got to the stoop there wasn't much shade left, so I had to squeeze over near the banister to get a little. Some little kids was playing sword fighting and using the garbage-can tops for shields. Every time the super came out the basement, he would make them put the tops back on the cans, and every time he went back in they would take them and play with them again.

Most of the people walking up and down the street was walking slow, talking to each other or saying something to the people just standing around. There wasn't too many people hurrying up, like they had someplace to go or something. Whenever somebody looked like they was in a hurry, everybody turned and looked at him. Sometimes they would try to guess where he was going. They would say things like "He probably trying to get his number in," or things like that. Mostly the street where Lonnie lived had a lot of people in it, especially in the afternoon when everybody was up and around.

Some of the people just hung around outside one of the buildings across the street. There was a store in one of the apartments, not a real store, but a place you could buy things like beer and cigarettes. Everybody knew everybody, too, because they was always there, and that made it nice. Some people who was around all the time started saying hello to me.

The street looked nice, with all the different colored people wearing different colored clothes. But if you looked up at the buildings, it looked different. Because the people downstairs was mostly moving around or walking. But upstairs people sat in the windows, and they didn't move much. A lot of the time the window people was old and afraid to come downstairs because somebody might bother them. You could tell if it was a old person, because you usually couldn't see all of them. They would be near the window, not hanging out of it, and all you could see was maybe an arm.

If a young person was looking out the window, then sometimes the people on the street would say something, especially if it was a girl.

"Hey, Mama, I sure would like to be doing *your* homework," the street person would say.

"You ain't been to school enough to be doing my homework, turkey!"

They would say something like that, or other things, and it would be nice to listen to it even though they wasn't talking to you or nothing. The street was nice, especially when it was real hot. In the house it felt like the heat was pushing in on me, and I had trouble breathing. It was hot outside, too, but at least on the outside, if a breeze did come along, you was right there to get it.

Two fat ladies had chairs which they was sitting in near the curb. Both of them had handkerchiefs, too, and they kept fanning themselves with them or wiping at their necks. I wasn't looking at them in particular, but I saw them fanning and wiping and sitting on their chairs trying to chase a dog away when Denise came and sat on the stoop, too. One of the women was doing some knitting, and she had sat right next to a fire hydrant and hung her bag on it. The dog went up near the fire hydrant and started sniffing around and the lady kept saying, "Choo! Choo!" and waving her handkerchief at the dog.

"You see Bubba?" Denise asked. I was surprised she remembered me because I had just met her once before.

"No," I said.

"Lonnie upstairs?" she asked. There was little drops of sweat on Denise's lip.

"No, he had to go downtown and take care of some business," I said. "You want a Twinkie?"

"No, I got a upset stomach."

We watched the dog walk away and then look back at the fire hydrant. Then he scrunched down real low and started sneaking up on the fire hydrant again. The fat lady was watching him, though, and was giving him a mean look. He got about a half a car away and then he turned and went.

"You live near here?" I asked Denise.

"Over on a Hundred-twenty-eighth Street. I used to live on a Hundred-twenty-sixth Street, but they tore it down. You Lonnie's boy, right?"

"Yeah." Denise was pretty. She had real dark skin and pretty eyes. Her eyes looked just a little bit Chinese, only they was very round and Chinese and not little and Chinese.

"Where was you living before?"

"Before I moved over here?"

"Yeah."

"With my grandmother. Then she got real sick, and then I had to come live over here."

"She die?"

"No."

"Then how come you had to come live over here?"

"'Cause she got old and she got sick."

"Oh. How old are you?"

"Twelve, almost thirteen."

"I used to be twelve."

"How old are you now?" I asked.

"About nineteen, going on twenty."

Denise nudged me and I looked over to where she was looking. The dog, who had went and laid down in the shade of a car, had got up and was looking over at the fire hydrant again. His tongue was hanging out the side of his mouth and his tail was stuck in between his legs. The two fat women was talking to themselves and wasn't paying no attention to the dog. Then the dog started walking, like he was going to walk right past the fire hydrant and not pay it no mind. But just as he was going by he turned around real quick and lifted his leg against the fire hydrant. Both of the women jumped up and started yelling, "Choo! Choo!" and waving their handkerchiefs. But it was too late. The dog had got the fire hydrant and one of the fat ladies' left foot.

Denise covered her face with her hands so the women wouldn't see the way she was laughing, and so did I. But across the street some other people had seen the dog, too, and they was laughing and pointing at the lady who got her foot peed on. Must have been a lot of people who was watching the dog, because a lot of people was pointing and laughing. The dog, he went on down the street minding his business.

When Denise had stopped laughing, she took her hands off her face and there was tears in her eyes from laughing. We watched the woman wipe off her shoe with a piece of newspaper and move her chair down a little way from the fire hydrant.

"What you mean—about nineteen?" I asked her.

"I'm eighteen," she said. "But then I'll be older and then I'll be about nineteen or twenty. When I get to be nineteen or twenty me and Bubba is gonna get married."

"Is that other girl going to marry Lonnie?" I asked.

"What other girl?"

"That girl that was upstairs yesterday when you was up there."

"Lois," Denise said. "That's Lois. No, she ain't gonna get married, just me and Bubba. We gonna live on Long Island or someplace like that and buy a house."

I kept talking to Denise and she talked kind of funny. She talked okay, in a way, and then in another way she didn't say things the whole way. She would say part of something and I knew that she knew what she was talking about, but I had to kind of piece things together to make sense of it. We sat on the stoop and talked for almost a whole hour, and she asked me if I wanted some more Twinkies, 'cause she would get some money and buy them for me. I said no, thanks. Before she left she said that she liked me. I liked her, too.

The mailman came and he put some mail in Lonnie's box. I knew where Lonnie kept the key to the mailbox, and I went upstairs and got it.

There was only two things in the mailbox. One was a thing about soap powder, a coupon, and the other was a letter from the welfare. It was a letter but I knew it was the check. I took it upstairs and put it on Lonnie's bed. I wanted to open it up and see if it was the check even though I knew it was. I thought about it for a while and then I thought I better put the check back in the mailbox. I don't know why Lonnie got two checks, but he had a way about getting mad if you asked him something he don't want to tell you so I put it back. I forgot to put back the soap powder thing but I figured it didn't make much difference anyway.

Later when Lonnie come home I saw him take the key and go back downstairs to the mailbox. I was reading a comic book when he got back upstairs. He didn't say nothing. He didn't even say that he got the check. The next day I saw the check in Lonnie's drawer when I went to get a pair of socks out. It still wasn't opened.

There was another month to go before school started and I didn't have much to do. Some of the counselors at the center started a basketball tournament and a tennis tournament. I didn't know how to play tennis and I couldn't play basketball that well, either. So mostly I hung around a lot, not doing much.

It rained for four days in a row and I had to stay inside most of the time except when Lonnie got mad at me and told me to go outside anyway. He didn't want me hanging around him too much, he said. I didn't mind hanging around him, though.

One thing he really hated was when I looked at him all the time. Sometimes I would look at him and think about how I look and try to imagine me looking just like him, or sometimes I would just imagine how I would look when I grew up.

"What you starin' at me for, man?" he would say when he caught me looking at him. Then I would say, "Nothing," or something like that. Then he would look at me real mean and keep staring at me even though I wasn't looking at him until I could feel his eyes looking at me. When I looked up he would be staring straight at me. It used to make me feel small because I didn't want him to be mad at me and I just couldn't help myself from looking at him. One time, though, he caught me looking at him and it happened kind of funny and we both laughed. It was the first time that we had laughed together.

I was looking at him but not straight at him. I was looking at him in the mirror out of the corner of my eye. He played ball a lot and he had hurt his ankle. He was sitting on the bed, fixing on his ankle. He put some tape around his ankle, and I watched him, and then, after a while, I noticed that his hands wasn't moving or fixing the tape any more. Then I looked up where his eyes was, and he was looking at me. Only this time instead of getting mad he smiled. And when he did that I smiled, too. He told me to stop looking at him and go on and fix him some tea or something. But he said it in a nice way and I felt real good about that.

On the last day that it rained I had went to the movies, and when I got home Bubba and Stone and Denise was at the house. At first I only saw Bubba and Stone sitting around the table talking to Lonnie. They had a brown envelope with herb in it and I knew they was going to smoke it, so I just said a "hi" to them and went into my room. That's where Denise was. She was sitting in my room reading a comic book. When I came in she reached into her pocket and pulled out some Lifesavers and gave me one. It was the fruit kind, which I liked. Denise and me sat in my room while Lonnie and Bubba and Stone talked outside. Sometimes we could hear them slap hands and me and Denise started playing slap hands, too, and she started giggling. Then I made believe I was smoking herb and she did, too. We almost got caught fooling around like that when Lonnie and Bubba came into the room. They told us they was going out for a while. Bubba told Denise to go home, and Lonnie said I could watch some television if I wanted to. I don't know why he said that because I always watched television anyway.

I watched television and then I almost fell asleep. It was sleep and then it wasn't sleep. I had a half dream about being in the Foreign Legion which was what I had seen on television. I was a officer and when I led my men into battle we was lined up behind a little hill. I was just about ready to tell them to charge over the hill to fight the enemy when I couldn't figure out who the enemy was. That woke me up, I guess. And even after I woke up I still could not figure out who the Foreign Legion was fighting against.

Anyway, when I woke up, the television was on and there was another movie on about a guy who was like a secretary to a lady. I was watching that when I heard Lonnie and them come in. They talked for a while and there was some bumping around and things and then I heard Stone and Bubba leave. I turned the television off and went on to sleep, but I don't remember dreaming again.

When I got up the next morning it was still kind of early and I figured Lonnie wasn't up. I got up and dressed and went out to the bathroom. On the way to the bathroom I saw a lot of stuff on the table. I saw Lonnie was still sleeping and so I took a good look at the stuff.

There must have been twenty or maybe twenty-five rings and some watches and things on the table. There was some other things, too, like ladies wore. I went back to bed and I stayed there. I had to go to the bathroom, but I didn't want Lonnie to know I had seen all that stuff. He didn't wake up for a long time, but somebody started banging on the door and that woke him up. It was Stone. They talked for a while, but I couldn't hear what they was saying. I really had to go to the bathroom bad, so I put on the television kind of loud so that they knew I was awake. I waited for another minute and then I went outside to the bathroom. I said, "Good morning," and Stone said, "Good morning, little brother," but Lonnie didn't say anything. The stuff on the table was gone.

When I come out of the bathroom, Stone was standing at the door talking to Lonnie and then he left. Lonnie told me to fix him some coffee.

"Where did all that stuff come from?" The words came out of me like I didn't even know they was in there.

"What stuff?" Lonnie leaned back against the table and crossed his legs.

"The stuff that was on the table before," I asked. My heart was beating so hard I could feel it in my neck.

"Why you want to know?"

"No reason," I said. I didn't even know I was going to ask about it.

"Now who you think stupid, me or you?" Lonnie came over to where I was still trying to get the teapot filled with water. He stood right next to me so his arm was touching mine. Then he leaned over and talked real soft in my ear "I ask you a question."

"I don't know," I said. I was so scared I forgot the question.

"Uh-huh. Yeah." Lonnie walked over and picked up the butcher knife and looked at me. "Some people too nosy for they own damn good. You know that?"

I nodded. Then he came over to me real quick, and I put my hand up so he wouldn't hit me in the face. But he just smiled and turned on the burner under the coffee.

The rest of the day I was too scared to even talk to Lonnie. Every once in a while he would look at me and smile. I didn't know where he got all those rings and watches and things. Maybe they wasn't even his. Maybe they belonged to Bubba, I thought, or even Stone. I thought a lot of things, but deep down I was thinking that somebody stole that stuff.

Bubba and Denise came by with Denise's friend Gloria. Gloria was about my age. She looked kind of nice. They all sat around for a while—Gloria was sitting with them, too. Then Denise and Gloria had to leave, and then Lonnie told Bubba that I had asked where they got the stuff. Soon as he said that I wanted to cry. I didn't like Bubba. Bubba was kind of light-skinned and he used to wear his hair back and he always looked like he was mad at somebody. His eyes wasn't white—they was yellow most of the time or kind of pinkish—and the middle part of his eyes, something like the irish, was light brown.

"Hey, he don't mean no harm, man," Bubba said. "My man just wants a little taste of the get-go. Right, little brother?"

I shrugged and kept on looking at television, making believe I was interested in it.

They kept on talking and then they was smoking herb and Lonnie was drinking, too. After a while Bubba left and Lonnie call me over next to him and told me to sit down with him on the bed. Then it was when I really couldn't stop crying, and I don't know why, only that things wasn't good at all. No, they wasn't good at all.

Lonnie started talking, and his breath smelled like wine, and I could smell the herb in the air, too. When he was talking his words come out wrong— not wrong, just messed up a lot from the drinking. I didn't even understand all the words he was saying, but I knew what he was meaning.

"See, you been thinking all your life about being a boy, dig?" He leaned against the headboard and looked at me, and his eyes was just half open. "But you got to start thinking about being a man. And being a man is all about not letting nobody take your manhood from you. See, if you let some sucker take your manhood from you, then you ain't no man. You a punk. I know all about that and I don't let nobody take my manhood.

"Now—" He stopped and poured some wine in the glass and then he drank out of the bottle. "Now, if they take something away from you, you got to take something back from them, see? You got to do that or you might as well let yourself get turned out. Because when it all come down it's about looking out for your manhood. Ain't nobody gonna look out for your manhood for you. You got to do that for yourself.

"And when you walking you got your manhood in what you got the same as you got it in what you be doing. If you ain't got nothing it's the same as being turned out because you ain't nothing but a punk. You go someplace and some cat look at you like you ain't nothing just because he got his thing together. What you think he saying, man? Huh? What you think he saying? He saying he got your manhood. That's what he saying. . . ."

He kept on talking about being a man and everything, but what he got around to saying was that all the stuff that was on the table was stole stuff. I just kept looking at him and looking at him while he went on talking and talking, and then he fell asleep.

I looked outside and thought about going out, but there wasn't nothing to do out there. A few guys was sitting around but there really wasn't nothing to do. I started feeling bad. "Acting like a dyin' calf in a thunderstorm!" Grandma Carrie used to say. I used to try to imagine being a dying calf in a thunderstorm and I couldn't, but I knew it must have felt bad.

After that me and Lonnie didn't have a whole lot to say to each other. He still walked around acting like he was mad at me all the time, but I didn't even care. He always left some money around for food, though.

I went to see Grandma Carrie again. I asked one of the nurses to tell her I was downstairs, like I always did. It took a long while for Grandma Carrie to come down, but she looked better than she had before. She asked me was I saying my prayers, and I lied and said yes. I figured I would ask God to forgive me later on.

"How you getting on with that father of yours?"

"Okay."

"What you mean, okay?" she said.

"I think he stole something," I said. Right away I figured maybe I shouldn't have said nothing.

"He gonna end up right back in that penitentiary!" Grandma Carrie was shaking her head. "He in any trouble now?"

"No, ma'am."

She just sat there and shook her head. I was sitting next to her, and she was kind of rocking back and forth and turning that thing around they put on her arm. When she got into the hospital they put a thing on her wrist with her name on it. She rocked and sometime she looked around like she was looking for something to come in the door.

When she said the part about Lonnie being in jail, something jumped in me. It was like I was wild inside for a minute. I never knew he had been in jail before, and I didn't know what to think about it too much. I was even a little scared of him, right then and there, even though he wasn't there. Just knowing he had been in jail was scary.

Grandma Carrie made a funny little noise and then started talking to herself like she did sometime, only I knew that she was talking to me the same time she was talking to herself.

"They's more than one kind of bread in this world," she said. "They's white bread and then they's black bread. Some of the time you get to eat the white and then some of the time you get to eat the black. Well, let me tell you, we all got to eat a little black bread sometime. And we got to learn to thank God for that, too. You hear that, Tippy?"

"Yes, ma'am," I said, sure glad she didn't ask me to explain it.

"You going to stumble more than once before you reach the grave, and the devil going to be right there to put a crutch under you. But when that happen you turn on away from the devil, you hear?"

"Yes, ma'am."

"Uh-huh." Grandma Carrie was turning the plastic thing on her wrist faster and faster. "When the devil offers you his crutch you just turn your eyes up to heaven and say, 'Precious Lord, take my hand, lead me on, let me stand.' Tell the Lord you're tired. Tell Him you're weak. And don't be afraid to tell Him you're worn, too. It ain't all for nothin', you know. You just don't walk this side of the vale for nothin'."

Then she said, "You say he stealing?"

"I'm not really sure," I said, trying to ease it off some.

"You know that stealing and carrying on ain't right," she said.

"I know."

"God can't stand a thief." Grandma Carrie went like she was spitting on the floor but nothing came out. "Ain't no true Christian person can stand a thief!"

She told me to save a few pennies up so I wouldn't have to depend on Lonnie to eat. She said she'd get out the hospital as soon as she could. Then I left and it was hard to go. On the way back to the block I asked God to forgive me for lying about saying my prayers. I decided to say a prayer, right then and there while I was walking down the street, but I couldn't. I was mad at God and I tried to push being mad out of my head. I tried to think of something else, like the baseball game or something like that, but I just thought about being mad. I didn't know why God made me live with Lonnie who stole people's things or why He got Grandma Carrie sick, but I knew I didn't like it. If I said I liked it, that would be a lie because I didn't. But it wasn't right to be mad at God, so I tried to push it out of my head.

Denise was sitting on the steps.

"Lonnie looking for you," she said.

"What he want?" I said. I had a mad look on, which was the way I felt even though I know I wouldn't of had it on when Lonnie was there, 'cause I was scared of him. He could beat me. He was my father and all, but I think he wouldn't even hit me like a father. I think he would beat me up. I had a friend named José, and his mother's boyfriend beat him up once.

"Stone got his uncle's car," Denise said. "We was driving around all morning."

"You and Stone?"

"Me and Stone and Lonnie and Bubba," she said. She was digging in her pocketbook and I knew she was going to come up with something to eat. It was a chocolate bar.

"No thanks."

"It ain't dirty!"

"You are!" I said. I stood up and sat on the other side of the stoop. Now I was mad at Denise and she hadn't done nothing but offer me some chocolate. I looked over where she was sitting and she was looking away. I went back over and sat next to her again and said I was sorry.

"That's all right!" she said in a happy kind of voice. Then she smiled a put-on smile.

I took part of the chocolate she still had in her hand 'cause I knew it would make her feel a little better.

Lonnie and Stone and Bubba came down and Bubba told Denise to go home and they told me to come with them. We got into Stone's uncle's car and just started driving around. We stopped at White Castle and got some hamburgers and French fries and then drove around some more. Stone and

Bubba was sitting in the front seat, and me and Lonnie was sitting in the back seat. I wasn't saying anything and Lonnie was just talking to Bubba and Stone. That was all right with me. They was smoking herb in the car and it was making me a little dizzy even though they had the window open.

Finally we stopped someplace in the Bronx and Lonnie and them got out. Bubba told me to sit in the front seat and blow the horn if I see anybody coming. He said that they were going to go into the store and sneak some potato chips. He gave me a little punch like it was supposed to be cool or something. I didn't know what to do—just sitting there like a dummy while they went in and snuck potato chips was stupid. If I saw a cop I wouldn't even blow the horn, I thought. I didn't see one, though. I looked over across the street where the grocery store was, and I could see Bubba standing near the door but I couldn't see Lonnie and Stone. I just started turning my head away when I saw Bubba move. When I looked back, Bubba was running towards the car and Lonnie and Stone was running right behind him. I moved over and I looked back again. Bubba got in and started the car up and Lonnie got in the back. Just as Stone was getting in I heard something going *pop, pop* and the windshield broke. Stone turned back towards the store, and he had a gun. I heard another *pop* and the glass in front of the store broke and then Stone jumped in the car and Bubba drove away as fast as anything. We went for about fifteen blocks under the elevator trains, then Bubba pulled the car over and said we had to get out of it.

"I got hit in my damn leg, man!" Stone said. I could feel my heart jumping in my chest. I looked down and saw the gun on the back seat between Stone and Lonnie. Lonnie saw me looking at it and pushed my face around. Then I looked straight ahead out the window.

"How bad is it?" Lonnie was saying.

"Think the sucker got a piece of the bone!" Stone said.

Bubba didn't say nothing—he just started the car up again and started down some streets that was catty-corner to the street where the elevator train ran. We drove slow and then we crossed the bridge and came back to where we lived. Bubba told us to get out and he was going to get rid of the car. Lonnie put the gun in his pants pocket, and me and him helped Stone up the stairs. When we got up there we put Stone on my bed. I looked at the clock-radio and saw that the whole thing didn't take no time because it wasn't hardly a hour since we left White Castle.

When we got through putting Stone on the bed, Lonnie gave him some whiskey, or maybe it was some wine, and he drank that. Then he said that maybe the guy didn't get the bone after all, and it wasn't nothing because he had two other bullets in him.

"Let's see it," Lonnie said.

Stone tried to pull his pants leg all the way up but he couldn't get it over his knee so he took his pants down. Stone was real dark in the face, but he was only brownskin on his legs. There was a bump on his leg where it was swelled up, and there was a hole right on top of the bump. It had bled some but not as much as I thought a bullet would make you bleed. Lonnie said it didn't look too bad. Then he took out a bag from his shirt, a little brown one, and gave it to Stone.

"Count this money," Lonnie said. "Come on with me, man."

I followed him out into the other room and we went into the bathroom.

"Stand in the corner."

I stood in the corner. I saw that he had the gun in his hand and I started crying. I was scared and my legs got weak.

"Turn around."

I was too scared to turn around, and he tried to

push me around, but I kept looking at the gun and wouldn't turn. He put his hand under my face and started digging his nails into me, but I still didn't turn around even though my face was hurting. Then he was saying something and I didn't know what it was at first, but then I heard him say to shut up and I tried to stop crying but I couldn't. We kept a bag in the bathroom for garbage and he pushed it in the corner. Then he flushed the toilet and while it was flushing he pointed the gun at the bag and shot it.

"You see that, sucker?" He held the gun up in front of me. "I can shoot your ass the same way and nobody even hear it. You open your mouth about this one time and you gonna be that garbage. You hear me?"

I said yes, and then he let me go out of the bathroom, but I had to go right back in a moment later to use the toilet.

That's about the time I got into a crying thing. Every time I looked around I'd be crying. Sometime I would catch myself crying and wouldn't even have a reason.

I didn't go to see Grandma Carrie either because I knew if I did I would just start crying again and then I'd have to tell her what happened or tell her a lie, which is what I would probably do.

But another thing I felt was kind of excited. I didn't like Lonnie pushing me around or anything, but the rest of it was kind of exciting. I kept on going between two things—no, really three things. One was hating on Lonnie and the other was not hating on him and the other one was being excited about everything. I kept on seeing it over and over again, like a movie inside me, and I even made believe that I was Stone. If I had got shot, then Lonnie would probably have fixed me up the way he was doing Stone.

"Hey, Tippy, I brought you something!" Lonnie
threw this big square package on the bed. "Open
it up."

I looked at it and saw there was a sales slip so I
figured he must have bought it for real. I picked it
up and it was light. I was a little nervous about
opening it up because I didn't think he was going
to buy me nothing. I opened it and saw it was a
basketball. Lonnie said to come with him and he
was going to show me how to play ball. I didn't
want to go, but he had been drinking, and he gets
mad if you just look at him wrong when he's been
drinking. So we went to the park.

There was some other guys there, a little older
than me, and he went up to them and asked if they
wanted to play against me and him. These two guys
said okay and we started playing. They was real
good and they could have beat us even if Lonnie
hadn't been drinking. But he was stumbling around
and things, and they started laughing. Some of the

guys watching the game started laughing, too. At first I was embarrassed, but then I got mad, real mad. I just wanted to shut them up. I played as hard as I could, but the harder I played the more we fell behind.

Lonnie had brought a bottle of wine in a paper bag and put it against the fence. When they was going to take the ball out, he would go over and get a quick drink, and then the other guys would crack up. He started making crazy passes and saying things to me like "How come you didn't get that?" and things like that. I just wanted to leave the park after a while. We started catching up a little but only because they would let Lonnie shoot the ball so they could crack up. Finally we lost.

On the way home he put his arm around my shoulder. I didn't mind as long as he didn't stumble or anything.

"My daddy never played ball with me," Lonnie said. "He used to be too busy. I used to have to go out by myself and maybe play with some of the other kids' fathers or by myself."

He sniffed, and I thought he was crying but he wasn't—he just sniffed. It was like a habit. Another habit he used to have was to put his hand between his legs and pull himself up. He did that a lot, especially when he was talking to somebody. I did it once, to see what it was like, and I couldn't see why he did it.

"You know how much that basketball cost?" he asked.

"No."

"Twenty dollars," he said. "What you think of that?"

"That's nice." I didn't really think nothing of it because I didn't want the ball.

He asked me if I wanted a drink, and I told him no. He said that it was okay to drink but not to fool around with herb and stuff like that. I said okay. We sat on the stoop for a while and he started falling asleep, not really falling asleep but almost. He would just about fall to sleep and then he would wake up all of a sudden. If he was saying something when he started falling asleep, he would wake up and finish just what he started to say. I shook him once and told him why didn't he go upstairs and lay down? He said okay, that it was good looking out. And then he left.

When he was gone I was thinking about how he looked, because I took a good look at him when he was dozing off. He didn't really look much like me after all.

That night I had a dream. The dream was so real I can remember every little part of it. I was dreaming that I was asleep and the doorbell rang and a man came with a telegram. Lonnie answered the door and the man gave him the telegram and it was for me. The telegram said that Grandma Carrie was out of the hospital and had went home, and that I could come home anytime I wanted to. It was late at night or maybe early in the morning when I got the telegram, and for a while I went back to bed and lay down and thought about going home to Grandma Carrie in the morning. But then I decided to go right then and I told Lonnie. Lonnie was taller than he really was, and he told me to go ahead if I wanted to, and he gave me one of the welfare checks that had come. I put the welfare check in a shopping bag with some clothes and I started to leave.

Lonnie asked me why I was going while it was still dark outside, and I said I just was, there was no reason. Then the funny part of the dream started. I started walking to Grandma Carrie's house and it looked like the longer I walked the further it was away. I kept walking and walking and it was always just a little further. Then I heard somebody calling my name and I looked back and there was only one other person on the whole street—it was Lonnie.

"Ain't you going to take your basketball?" he said.

I said that I was going to leave it at his house so I could play with it when I came over and he said okay. Then I started walking again and I never did seem to get there. Then I started jogging, and even running, but I never could get to Grandma Carrie's house. That was the whole dream. I didn't dream anything else.

The next day I walked over to Grandma Carrie's house and it wasn't that far.

I didn't go out a lot because I was thinking that if somebody saw me in the car when Lonnie and them took that money they might say, "Hey, he was in the car!" and then start chasing me or shooting at me. When I did go out sometimes, I would just sit on the stoop or go to a movie if I had any money.

I went to see Grandma Carrie and I learned something that I didn't know before. It made me feel really bad. I had thought that she was going to get all right and come home soon, but now I knew that she was going to be in the hospital a long time. When I was downstairs waiting for her to come down, I saw the nurse that had let me go up and visit with her when she first went in the hospital, and I asked her how long she thought she would be in.

"She ain't sick, boy," the nurse said. "Your grandmother is just plain old, and the only thing that stops that is dying."

The nurse went on and started talking to the policeman that stayed in the hospital all the time, and then she came back and said that she was sorry, that she didn't want to make me feel bad. I said that was all right. I didn't know what else to say.

When Grandma Carrie came downstairs, she was mad. At least she looked like she was mad, and at first I thought it was because I hadn't come around like I told her I would before. Then I found out that she wasn't mad at me.

"Some people got so much nerve it ain't even funny!" she said.

"What do you mean, Grandma?"

"That little dried-up hussy!" Her lips was tight together and she was breathing heavy. "You saw that little hussy over there in the corner near the window?"

I nodded that I did, but I didn't really remember seeing anybody over in that corner.

"I got two magazines from them gray ladies, or whatever you call them. I got me *Ebony* and I got me *Good Housekeeping*. I go to the bathroom and when I got back Miss Thing done got my magazine and got her nose stuck up in it! It made me so mad I felt like pulling the little bit of hair she got left right out by the roots!"

"She wouldn't give it back when you asked?"

"Ask? Ask what?" Grandma Carrie looked at me up and down. "Ask what? I wouldn't ask that hussy for a drop of water in a middle of the desert! That's all she waiting for, me to come up and ask her for *my* magazine. I will never read another magazine on this side of the grave, and God is my secret judge if I'm lying, before I'd ask that hussy for one."

Grandma Carrie went on talking about the woman who took her magazine. We sat for a long time, mostly her talking and me listening, and I didn't know her like I used to know her. She was being like somebody else. I felt sorry for her, in a way, and in another way I didn't. I mean I felt sorry for the Grandma Carrie that I used to know, but I didn't feel sorry for her now that she was different. Her hands had got bigger, too, swoll up around the knuckles. She walked about the same.

7

I was sitting on the stoop again, mainly because I didn't have no money, when Billy, Pedro, Didi, and two other girls I didn't know come up. Lonnie and Stone was on the stoop, too, waiting for Jack, the numbers man. Every day they used to pick out their numbers and bet them with Jack when he came around.

Jack was a little weasel-face guy. You would tell him your numbers, and he would turn his head to one side so his ear would be near you, and every time you would say a number he would give a little nod with his head and then he had the number. He never wrote no numbers down, so he could never be arrested for it.

"Where you going?" Lonnie asked Pedro.

"To the roof to do some star watching," Pedro said. "And you see we brought our own stars along."

"Yeah. You got three stars and two dudes," Lonnie said. "Who gonna work overtime?"

"I think I can handle it." Pedro looked at his hands and tried to be cool. He was about fourteen, but he had dropped out of school and had a job working on a bread truck.

"Why don't you take Tippy on up with you?"

"C'mon on, Tip-Tip." Pedro slapped my knee. "You look like you can be a good star watcher."

I didn't want to go to the roof with them, but I knew if I didn't Lonnie was going to get into all that manhood stuff again. He was always saying what it meant to be a man and all. So I ended up going up on the roof with them.

Billy was carrying a bag and he opened it up and he had three bottles of this stuff that tastes like milk shakes but has whiskey in it. He also had some paper cups, and we sat around and started drinking this stuff. It was good. Some of it was strawberry and some was banana.

"Tippy, this is Juanita, Juanita—Tippy." Pedro introduced us and we said hello to each other. Then he introduced me to the other girl, whose name was Sheila. That was his girlfriend.

"What happened to that other chick—you know." Billy snapped his fingers in front of Didi like it was supposed to make her remember who the other girl was. "That girl wear them funny glasses."

"Dolores?"

"Yeah! I thought she was supposed to be hanging out."

"She went to Confession Sunday."

"Again?"

"Ain't nothing wrong with going to Confession!" Didi's voice got higher.

"All she do is party when she want and then go to Confession so she can start again."

"No, she don't either, she's serious."

"Can't nobody just forgive your sins, anyway!" Billy poured some more of the drink in his cup and some more in mine. "If you go out here and kill somebody, how some sucker gonna just . . . gonna just say . . . hey, man, it's okay."

"He don't say no 'hey, man, it's okay,'" Didi said. "You go in and you say, 'Forgive me, Father, for I have sinned.' And then you tell what sins you done and then you get forgiven. But you don't get forgiven unless you believe in it and mean it with your whole heart."

"Whether *you* mean it or not don't make no difference," Billy said.

"Preach, brother." Pedro put his arm around Sheila and leaned back against the wall.

"The only thing is happening is that some guy done forgive you, that's all," Billy went on. "Do you hear God saying, 'I forgive you, too'?"

"Anybody ever tell you that you're about as ignorant as you are ugly? The damn *priest* is there doing God's will, turkey!"

"And that ain't what you got to worry about anyway," Pedro said. "What you got to worry about is when you die and go to heaven and can't find the door the niggers is supposed to come in."

"Everybody in heaven is going to be the same," Sheila said. "That's what I believe."

"If you black when you die, you gonna be black when you get to heaven," Billy said.

"You ever seen the inside of a church?" Didi asked Billy.

"I didn't ask for your two cents," Billy said without looking at her.

"Well, I'm gonna give you my two cents and you can take it right to your mama, okay?"

"Say what!" Billy jumped up and made a fist.

"You feel froggish you leap right on over here, baby," Didi shot back. "You'll have more than ears upside your head."

Billy looked at her mean for a while, and then he sat back down. I didn't think she looked that tough, but he sat down anyway. Then Didi started talking.

"You can go to Confession and if you believe in

your heart that you are truly sorry God'll forgive you. Then you say them little things you got to say and cut out whatever it was you was doing wrong, and if you died right then you'll go straight to heaven. And God ain't got no color. He's just a spirit."

"Hey, Billy, she got to be right," Pedro said. "'Cause if the white folks found out that God was black they'd be trying to move to a new neighborhood. Talking about property values and whatnot."

"That is about as funny as dog-do," Sheila said. "You'd better watch yourself. They got some equal opportunity just waiting for your ass down in hell."

"I don't have to watch myself, baby," Pedro said. "'Cause God sees what's in my heart and I got a pure heart."

"That's what my grandmother used to say," I said.

"Give Tip-Tip another drink." Pedro pushed one of the bottles towards me. "He's got the intelligence to agree with the master—namely, me."

We sat up on the roof and drank until all the bottles was empty. I got real dizzy but I decided not to let anybody know. I could look at Pedro and Billy and see them for a while, but then I wouldn't be looking at them so I could see them. They would just be there and I could see them, but I wouldn't be really looking at them. Then Pedro said that he and

Sheila were going over to her mother's house. Billy tried to get Didi to let him come over to her house, but she went someplace instead. I went on down to the house, and Lonnie saw that I had been drinking and couldn't walk so straight. He started laughing but not in a mean way like he usually did. He told me to lay down and even took my sneakers off. I fell asleep then and didn't wake up until almost eight-thirty. I had a bad headache but I stayed up and watched a movie.

Down from where we lived was a church, and sometimes I used to walk by it on the way over to Morningside Park. I didn't go to Morningside Park much since a guy got killed in there. He was playing basketball and another guy who he had a fight with shot him and killed him. But I knew where the church was, and a Spanish girl I used to know always went there, and she had Confession, too. I wasn't a Catholic or anything like that but I wondered if God would forgive me my sins if I went there and confessed them.

I wasn't too sure what my sins were. Grandma Carrie used to say that if you enjoyed the fruits of evil, then you was evil. I was at the holdup but I didn't know that they was going to do it. Sometimes I thought about if they had shot somebody in the store or killed them even, but I didn't want to think about it much. I used to push it out of my mind. I could push a lot of things out of my mind, not even think about them. Another thing I could do that I couldn't do when I stayed with Grandma Carrie—that was to go to sleep just about anytime I wanted to. I couldn't go to sleep when I stayed with Grandma Carrie unless it was late and there was nothing to do. Now I could go to sleep real easy.

I didn't think much about what I was going to do when I went to the church. I just walked in and looked around. It was about two o'clock or maybe a little later when I went in.

"Hello, may I help you?" The priest was tall and he scared me a little because I didn't see where he came from. He was white, or maybe Spanish.

"I was just looking," I said.

"For anything in particular?"

"You really have a box for people to confess in?"

"You ever been to Confession?" he asked. He didn't look old but his hair was gray on the sides.

I told him I had never been to Confession before, and he asked me if I was a Catholic and I said no to that, too. Then he asked me what I wanted to be when I grew up, and I said maybe a artist. He asked me if I wanted to make Confession.

"Sometimes it makes you feel good," he said. "Come on, let's go into the office."

We went into the office and he sat behind a desk and asked me things like what church I belonged to and who I lived with and did I miss my grandmother.

"What kind of things do you think you want to confess, Tippy?" He had a nice voice, like a teacher.

"I don't know."

"Well, do you think you live a good life?"

"I guess so."

"Is there anything you would like to talk about?" He said that after we had been quiet for a while.

"Can you confess somebody else's sins?"

"I think that might be a bit difficult," he said. "Some of your friends commit sins, you think?"

"Yeah, some of them."

"What do you think of the things they do?"

"I don't think it's right," I said. "Especially not with guns 'cause you could kill somebody."

"Guns? Just how old are these friends of yours, anyway?"

"Grown." I started thinking about Lonnie and Bubba and Stone, and I thought maybe I'd better not say anything too much.

"Well, I presume they stuck up a place," he said.

"Did you tell the police?"

"I think I better go."

"No, don't go," he said. "Let me get some books and things for you to read and think about, and maybe we can talk some other time. Stay here for a while."

He got up and went out of the office. There was a sign on his desk which said Father Morrow. There was a big clock on the wall, the kind they have in the George Bruce Library, and it was after three o'clock. I waited for a while, and then I got tired of waiting because I was just sitting in this office by myself. I wondered where Father Morrow was. I went outside the office and I saw him in a office just across from where I was, talking on the telephone. He was looking away from me. Otherwise I would have just waved at him or something and left, because I didn't want to wait no more. I went up to him to touch him on the arm so he would know I was leaving.

"Yes, he's about twelve or thirteen and he's talking about some grown friends of his robbing a place with a gun. I don't know where he lives except that it's in this neighborhood and—just a minute . . ."

He saw me standing there. Then he smiled at me and swallowed, and I thought he must have been talking about me to get me in trouble or he wouldn't have swallowed like that, like he was telling a lie or something.

"I'm going."

"Tippy, why don't you wait for a minute? I'll be right with . . ."

I didn't want to wait or anything. I went on down the hall to where the side of the church was and left. I turned back to see what he was doing, and he was pointing at me, and some other boys, mostly white but a few black, was looking at me. I cut out. I jumped down the steps and ran up St. Nicholas Avenue. I looked back again and they was running after me. When I got to St. Nicholas Park I cut up the steps going in the park. I didn't want to run across to my house because they would have known where I lived. They ran up the steps into the park after me. When I got to the top of the steps I looked again and only three boys was chasing me. One was white and the other two looked like they was either Spanish or black—I couldn't tell. I kept running through the park and I had to slow down a little and walk past a dog, but then I kept going. I ran all the way up to where the sledding place is, down that steep hill, and I started running down there when one of them caught up with me and grabbed the collar on my shirt.

I knocked his hand away and he hit me in the face with his fist. I pushed him in his face, and the other boy, the white one, caught up, and while I was pushing the first boy I kicked the white boy. The white boy jumped back and I could see the rest of them coming. Then I just started swinging with all my might, and I hit the first boy in the face and he fell down, and then I made like I was going to hit the white boy and he leaned back and I kicked him on the same leg I kicked him on before. They backed off of me and I started on down the hill again. The others came up and they threw a couple of rocks and a stick but they didn't follow me down the hill. They were calling me names, though, like thief and robber and stuff like that.

First I went down the hill, and then I went up St. Nicholas all the way to where the subway stop is on 135th Street. Then I cut down to Eighth Avenue and walked back to the block. I kept looking around to make sure that no one was following me or anything, and nobody was.

I went upstairs and nobody was there. I looked in the mirror and saw that my lip was busted up where that boy hit me. I hoped he would die. I kept looking at myself in the mirror, and at first I didn't like the way my lip was puffed up and all out of shape, but then I begin to like it because it was the way I was feeling inside. Not all puffed up and swollen but like a beat-up-looking guy.

One time when I got beat up and come home crying, Grandma Carrie made me pray to God and thank Him that I wasn't hurt real bad, and then I had to pray for the boy that beat me up and tell God that I was sorry about fighting. I thought about that, and all I could think about was that I was still mad at God. I had only went to church and thinking maybe to confess my sins and things like that when I get chased around and hit in the lip. I didn't get down on my knees or nothing—I just sat on the foot of Lonnie's bed and talked to God the best I could.

"God, that just ain't right. I didn't do nothing wrong and You know that. How come You doing me wrong? You got Grandma Carrie sick and in the hospital acting funny, You got my father doing bad things and nothing bad is happening to him, and I'm doing pretty good and everything bad is happening to me. This is *me*, God, this is Tippy. I ain't done nothing wrong!"

I knew that God could just strike me down dead or turn me into salt like He did somebody, but I was just so mad I didn't know what to do. I hung out in Lonnie's room and watched television, and then he came home. He said hi and I said hi. Then he come over to me and put his hand under my chin and push my face up and looked at it.

"What happened?"

"I had a fight with some boys."

"Where?"

"In the park."

"They take your money?"

"No, they was trying to catch me."

"What they trying to catch you for?" he said. "You want some fried chicken? I'm gonna go out and get some."

"No."

"What they trying to catch you for?"

"I don't know."

"You get any of them back?"

"I got two of 'em back good."

He stood and looked at me like he didn't know me or something, and then he ask me again about why they was trying to catch me, and I told him the whole thing.

"You did what?"

"You heard what I said."

I didn't even see him swing or anything. The only thing I knew was something hit me in the back of the head and I saw stars for a while. I went to get up and he hit me again in the stomach and again near my ear. He kept on hitting me. He kept

8

I had been looking around, trying to figure out what I should do, and I was standing near to where you go down into the subway when this guy came up to me. He was about the same size as me, except that he was light skin. He was a light brown skin, not yellow.

"Hey, man, you a punk?"

"Who, me?" I asked.

"Who I talking to if I ain't talking to you?" he said.

"No."

"What you doing?"

"Nothing," I said.

"What's your name?" he asked. He had this way of turning his head to one side when he talked. Also, he wore this big cap that was broke down on the side, and I figured he wanted to look tough. Grandma Carrie said that you never had to worry about nobody who was trying to look tough because it only meant they wasn't.

on punching me and punching me and my head was dizzy and I had some blood in my mouth. At first I tried to get away and then I just kept standing there. He hit me and knocked me on the bed and I got up and wished that he would just kill me so I could die.

"You tell them where I live?" He started shaking me but I couldn't even talk 'cause I couldn't get my breath, and then he just pushed me away in the corner. He ran out of the door and I could hear him running downstairs, and I hoped he would fall down or something. But then he came back up.

"You tell them where I live?" He put his hand on my neck and pushed me against the wall. I could hardly move my head but I shook it no.

He said that if the cops came to the house the first thing he would do was to kill me. He kept asking me if I understood that and I said yes. I wanted to tell him that I didn't care, too, but he would just only start beating on me again. I went to bed and thought about what happen, and I knew that God was getting back at me for being mad at Him and then I told God I was sorry and I tried to get the bad thoughts out of my mind. I told God that it was all right with me if He made me die.

My face took a long time to go down. I didn't go

out at all and I stayed in my room unless Lonnie was out. Then I would go into his room and see if there was anything to eat in the refrigerator. If there was I would eat something and if there wasn't I just wouldn't eat anything. All I really wanted to do was to sleep all the time.

When I did go out I saw Pedro. I asked him where he had bought those drinks that time and what he called them. He told me you had to know somebody to get them and he took me to a liquor store on Eighth Avenue. We went in, and Pedro told the man what we wanted, and he put it in a bag, and I gave him the money that I had. Lonnie didn't know I had the money, but it was what I had put away in case he didn't buy food, like Grandma Carrie had told me to do. We had to carry the bottles out of the liquor store in a box so that it looked like we was just there to get some boxes. I had bought three bottles and I gave one to Pedro and I took the other two home.

Lonnie was bringing a new girlfriend to the house a lot now. Sometimes she would stay all night and they would fool around. Once in a while he would say he was going out and not to let anybody in, and I knew that meant that he was going to be out all night long. When he was out all night long, he and his new girlfriend would come home

in the morning and then she would go to work. She was a nurse or something. I knew Lonnie would be out all that night so I didn't even hide the drinks. I put the television on and first I drank the chocolate drink and then I started drinking the strawberry drink. I didn't think of anything much by the time I got to the strawberry drink, and I must have fallen asleep because when I woke up the television was still on, only it didn't have a picture. I got up and went to the bathroom and I was kind of wobbly, so instead of taking my clothes off and going to bed I just lay down with them on and went to sleep again.

The next day when I woke up I had a headache again, just like the first time that I had some drinks. Only this time it was worse. It was like I had been beat up all over again. I threw up a little, too, but not much.

Later in the day I went over to see Grandma Carrie but the nurse said she was asleep and I should come back later. I started to but instead I went downtown to 42nd Street and just hung around. There's where I met Motown.

"Why?" I asked.

He didn't say nothing but just went over near the newspaper stand and leaned against the wall. At first I started just to go on into the subway like I was going to do in the first place, but then I figured I might as well talk to him because I really didn't want to go home.

"Tippy, my name is Tippy," I said.

"Tippy? What kind of a name is that?" he asked.

"That's the name my mother gave me," I said. "A lot of people think it's a nickname or something but it's not."

"It's okay."

"What's your name?"

"Motown."

"Motown?"

"Yeah. That's not my real name, but I don't be telling everybody my real name. Only about three people know my real name."

"Who?"

"Why you want to know?" he asked.

"I don't even care," I said.

"Just my friends know my real name," he answered. "Where you live?"

"You know where the Florsheim Shoes are on the corner of a Hundred-twenty-fifth Street?"

"No."

"Well, I live up from there on St. Nicholas," I said. "Where do you live?"

"Here, there, everywhere."

"Around here?"

"Around where?"

"Forty-second Street."

"No, man." He looked at me as if I had said something wrong. "Only freaks be living around here. I just hustle around here, that's all. What you doing down here?"

"Nothing to do."

"You go to school?"

"In the winter."

"You got any money?"

"Why?"

"Because I'm thinking about going over to Nathan's for a hot dog, but I ain't got no money to be buying you nothing," he said. "Hey, Victor! You still got them umbrellas?"

He was talking to a guy who was walking by, and the guy made an "O" with his fingers like everything was okay.

"That's my man, Victor," Motown said. "He gets stuff to sell and you get part of the money if you sell the things for him. You want to go over to Nathan's and get something to eat?"

I said okay. We started walking over towards

Broadway. I felt around in my pocket and found my three dollars. When Motown wasn't looking I took one dollar out of one pocket and put it in another pocket, just in case. But by the time I got to Nathan's I really liked Motown.

He had a dollar and I had three dollars so I bought the frankfurters. We messed around for a while and then he showed me how to sneak into a movie. We sneaked into the New Amsterdam and saw some movie about a bridge. It was a war movie and it was okay, but they always had pictures of the person's whole head. When the movie has pictures of a person's whole head, when they have that a lot, then it's a talky picture and I don't like it. When we got out of the picture he said he had to make some money so he could buy some food and he asked me if I wanted to make some. I said okay and we went down to a park near the library. He saw a man he knew and he asked him to loan him two dollars, and the man said he didn't have two dollars, but Motown wouldn't go away, he kept asking. The man was trying to talk to another boy who looked a little older than us. Finally he gave Motown two dollars and me two dollars. I was just standing there and hadn't asked for anything.

"How come he gave me two dollars?" I asked.

"Because he knew if he didn't I might kick his ass," Motown said.

We went on the subway and went out to where Motown lived. I thought the place I lived in was bad, but the place Motown lived in was even worser. It wasn't so bad-looking from the outside, almost as good as the place where Lonnie and me lived except some of the windows was covered up with tin. When we went inside it was bad, though, because no one hardly lived there except some bummy-looking guys who lived on the first floor and Motown who lived on the second floor. We bought some shrimp fried rice with the money we got from the man, and we ate that and then we sat around and talked. Motown didn't go to school even when school was going on. He said he didn't think school was too good for him because he wasn't book-smart.

"This guy told me once that they's two kinds of being smart. They's book-smart and then they's street-smart. He said I'm street-smart."

I told him that I wasn't too street-smart but I was a little book-smart and I could draw real good. He said that was hand-smart. I told him about the drinks I had, and he asked me if I wanted to buy some and I told him yes. I did, too. Because that made me feel like I didn't care for nothing. He and me went down to a place on Macon Street, near where he lived, only we went to a candy store that sold the same kind of drinks that I had got with Pedro. Motown said that sometime he drank them but sometime he drank just regular whiskey. We bought it and went back to the place where Motown lived and we just sat around and drank and talked.

"Who you live with?" he asked. I could hardly see him. There wasn't much light left outside and he was sitting in a corner. I had asked him before if he had a flashlight and he showed me two that he had, plus a whole lot of batteries. Then he showed me how he could change the batteries with his eyes closed.

"I live with my father," I said.

"He a chump?"

"He's okay."

"Where's your mother?"

"Dead," I said. "She died when I was a baby. You got parents?"

"What's that supposed to mean?"

"What's what supposed to mean?"

"That mess about having parents," he said. "What I look like—I come out of a damn egg or something?"

"No, I mean do you live with your parents?"

"I told you I live here."

"Oh."

"My parents broke up," he said. "My mother lives over on Gates Avenue and my father he lives with a woman on Dean Street."

"How come you don't live with your mother?" I asked.

"'Cause she's a chump!" Motown said. "She's always out messing around and that kind of thing. Sometimes I go over to see her. If she ain't got nobody there I stay over, but mostly she's got somebody there."

"How about your father?"

"You the F.B.I.?"

"No."

"Then how come you ask so many questions?"

"Just talking."

"What's your father like?"

"He's okay."

"He take you around?"

"Not much."

"What he do?"

"Like what?"

"What kind of work he do?" He got up and got one of the flashlights and put it on. Then he set it in the middle of the floor on its end. There was a bright circle of light on the ceiling with a bigger circle around it that wasn't so bright. I could see Motown pretty good then—he was scrunched up in the corner.

"He works on a truck," I said.

"What kind of truck?"

"A pie truck," I said, not really sure why I was saying that. "He delivers pies to stores and things."

"I bet you get all the pies you want, right?"

"Yeah."

"That's the joint, man. That's really okay."

Motown really seemed pleased when I told him that my father worked on a pie truck. I was glad that I told him that but kind of sad that I lied.

"He ever hit you or anything?"

"Sometimes."

"When you mess up or just when he want to?"

"About fifty-fifty."

"That how come you was messing around forty-deuce?"

"Forty what?"

"Forty-second Street."

"I guess so."

"If my father tried to beat on me I'd cut his ass," Motown said. "I don't take no beating."

"You can't beat your father," I said.

"Naw. He's a little sucker, too," Motown said. "But he hit you like a mule, Jim."

"My father don't hit too hard but it hurts just the same," I said. "Anyway, it makes me feel bad."

"That's 'cause you still a baby. You get on the street awhile and it won't even hurt. The only thing be hurting you is that you can't get back at the sucker. The hits come on you and you stand there and look him right in the eye, and then it won't even hurt."

"You can get used to it but it'll still hurt," I said.

"It won't hurt—you just wait and see," he said. "You know, if I was your father I wouldn't take you no place, either. You know why?"

"Why?"

"'Cause your eyes too big. Anybody ever tell you about your eyes, man? You stare at somebody you give them the shakes."

"You ain't too good-looking yourself."

"I'm better-looking than you!"

"No, you ain't."

"I got a little brother who look like you," Motown said. "He's ugly, too. You got any brothers?"

"No."

"When he gets a little bigger I'll probably take him around and things. Teach him the ropes. Tell him about girls and things. You ever fool around with a girl?"

I said no and asked him if he had and he said yes. Then I asked him what it was like and he said he couldn't tell me.

"How come?" I asked.

"You might get excited," he said.

"Get out of here."

"You too young, your heart couldn't take it." Motown was smiling and I smiled, too.

"If you get a letter do it come here?" I asked.

"I don't get no letters," he said. "Do you get letters?"

"No, not mostly. But if I write away for something, then I used to get it at my grandma's house."

"What did you write away for?"

"Anything free."

"How come?"

"To get a letter."

"That's pretty hip, man," Motown said. "You may be bug-eyed but you're kind of smart, too. You send away for them things in the paper and stuff, right?"

"Uh-huh."

"Yeah, that's hip. But I might get into trouble if I do that. You know, I'm wanted in three states, so I can't be putting my name and address around all over the place."

"What you wanted for?"

"I can't tell you," he said. "You might turn me in for the reward. That's why I don't let people know too much about me. You one of the few people who know my real name is Frank."

I didn't even know his real name was Frank, but I guess it just kind of slipped out. I liked him, though, and I didn't even believe he was wanted in three states. He was okay and I thought we could be friends. I slept there that night. I woke up in the middle of the night because I heard this funny sound. It scared me real bad at first. It was coming from the corner. I got the flashlight and turned it towards the corner. It was Frank, he was scrunching even further into the corner. He was all balled up and making a little noise, not like crying or anything, more like he was having a dream he didn't like. I thought about waking him up so he wouldn't have to finish the bad dream, but then he stopped making the noises and so I didn't. I went back to sleep and when I woke up he was gone. I was just putting my sneakers on when he came back with two egg sandwiches and some coffee for us. That's when I said we could probably be friends, and he said no, he didn't think so.

We hung out all day long and had a good time. Frank showed me how to get into three different movies without paying. I knew it was sorta like stealing but I didn't pay too much mind to it. Another thing he did was to put toilet paper in some machines like soda machines and like a machine that gave you cakes. Then later he would go take the toilet paper out and some money would be in there. He marked his machines with his name so everybody would see it and not be messing with it. He showed me where to look for a name to see if the machine belong to somebody already.

When it started getting dark he told me he had a lot of things to do and I better go on home. I asked him again if we could be friends, and he said he was too busy, he didn't have no time for friends. He said I was all right, though, and if I saw him again I could still call him Frank. Then he said he had to go and he went on. We was on 42nd Street and there was a lot of people doing this and that and mostly just being around. So when Frank walked away I couldn't see where he went.

I got on the subway. I was waiting for the train when I thought how all day me and Frank was sneaking on the subway without paying, but soon as he left I paid. Part of the way home I thought about Frank—he knew a lot of things and some of them was okay and some not okay but he wanted to show them to me and I was glad about that. I kept hoping that nothing bad was going to happen to him. I think we could have been friends if he didn't have too many things to do.

The second part of the trip home, mostly near the end, I thought about Lonnie. I was thinking that he would ask me where I was and stuff and maybe even hit me, but I wouldn't tell him no matter how hard it hurt. It was the first time in my life I spent a whole night out and I thought he would be real mad. He wasn't too mad. He asked me where I been. Instead of not saying nothing I told him I was at my friend Motown's house. Then he asked me did I eat up all the eggs.

I was thinking about Motown when I went to bed. I wanted to hang out with him mostly because he was somebody to hang out with. Going around in the subway was okay if I was with him, but I didn't think I could do it by myself too good. I thought about taking the Johnson brothers downtown and showing them where Motown had made his marks and stuff. I wouldn't call him Frank in front of the Johnson brothers, I'd call him Motown.

I liked telling Lonnie that I had spent the night at my friend's house because I heard him saying something to Stone, or maybe it was Bubba, about me not having friends. That was kind of true, that

I didn't have many friends. During the summer I didn't have many friends, but when I went to school I had a lot of friends that I hung out with. I knew if Frank did become my friend it would be like Mrs. Lilly and Grandma Carrie. They wasn't very much like each other but they was both old. Me and Frank wasn't very much like each other, either, except we didn't have nobody else. I figured that was as good a reason for having a friend as any other.

When I woke up it was still dark but I couldn't sleep. So I just lay in the bed and didn't do nothing. I started pretending a few things, like me and Frank being baseball players, things like that. I had to go to the bathroom, but then I heard Lonnie fooling around in the other room so I didn't go out. After a while they had stopped and I went out and went to the bathroom. When I was coming back from the bathroom I looked on Lonnie's bed and saw that he was asleep. Then I looked at who was in the bed with him and I give a jump 'cause I thought it was Grandma Carrie at first, but it wasn't. It was another lady and she was the same brown as Grandma Carrie and she was real thin. She was not old but not too young, and she must have knowed I was there because she sat up in bed and we was looking at each other like animals fixing to fight. I didn't know what to say and I hoped that she wouldn't tell Lonnie. I went on back in my bed.

When it got light out, they was making noises

like they was fixing to eat breakfast and I went out and said good morning. Lonnie, he said good morning but she didn't say nothing. She kept looking at me and she was trying to fix herself up and things like I was going to look at her or say something about her. Lonnie said there was some more grits left, and I took some and put butter on them, but the lady was looking at me so hard I couldn't even eat the grits. I ask Lonnie if he had any extra money, and he said wait till he go put his numbers in. He just had to go downstairs on the stoop, and he rushed downstairs before the numbers man came.

The lady was still there and she kept looking at me, and then she started in to ask me questions like what my name was and did I go to school. I didn't say much, though, because I didn't know why she was acting funny. It was Lonnie's house, not mine. When Lonnie got back he gave me a dollar and I left. The last thing I saw was that lady looking at me as I walked out the door.

I didn't know what to do so I just walked around for a while. I went up and saw Jack the numbers man standing at the subway taking people's numbers as they went to work. I stood and talked with him awhile, and he gave me another dollar. So I had two dollars that Lonnie and the numbers man give me but only one left-over dollar that I had been saving. No stores was open except the liquor stores and I didn't even think about it when I walked in.

"Strawberry." Strawberry was sweeter than banana, coconut, vanilla, and a lot sweeter than chocolate. Pedro said that he liked coconut the best because he liked odd things. The man in the liquor store went to the front and looked around before he let me leave. There was only some people waiting for the bus.

"You take that *medicine* right home to your mother now," he said. He looked at the people waiting for the bus and winked his eye, and they all laughed because they knew it was a liquor store, not a medicine store.

I went over to the park and started drinking the drink. I wasn't thinking much again, but this time I noticed that I wasn't thinking of much. It was kind of funny and I tried to think about thinking about a lot of things, and that was hard to do. Then I watched some people get on a bus, the kind that takes you to picnics and things. They was carrying bags with their lunches in it and I wished I was going with them. Some of them had baseball bats and gloves, too. Then I started thinking about how me and Frank were ballplayers. The other outfielders besides me and Frank was Mickey Rivers and Reggie Jackson. I don't know how there got to be four outfielders.

I was drinking the drink and not feeling too bad when it was almost all gone, but I had to go to the bathroom. I went behind a tree but when I stood up I could hardly hold still. The ground was spinning and I had to hold onto the tree. Before, when I had had a lot of drinks and I got dizzy, I laid down and went to sleep, so I laid down again but I wasn't sleepy and my stomach started to bother me. I thought maybe I had better go home.

The ground looked like it was moving around when I tried to get across the street, and I fell and could hardly get up. Some people was looking at me, too, and I felt embarrassed. I tried to hurry up but I still couldn't walk good, and a boy was standing on the sidewalk and he was laughing at me, and I was mad. Then I didn't know how much time I was taking because I saw things and almost saw me do things like turn around with the sun in my eyes, and there was a garbage can on the sidewalk and the people was all getting didn't want to step in no dog mess bus so I thought maybe I would sit down for a while and I push this boy in his face. Then he push me and I was going to fight him when somebody else grab me and say, "Go on," but I couldn't even go on like he said and they was going away like the picture on a television when you turn it off but it don't go right away and then it was gone and then I couldn't go on like it was off with the picture gone. . . .

When I woke up I was in a house and a ball game was on television. I was scared at first and I started to get up fast, but a pain got me in the head. It was so hard that I thought somebody had hit me with something, but it was inside my head.

"How you feeling, man?"

I looked up and there was this real big guy sitting in a chair watching television. I started to get up again and I got the pain in my head and he came over to where I was laying.

"Take it easy, now," he said. He laid me back down, and then I heard footsteps and a woman come in. She was a big woman, too. Not so big but a little fat.

"Want me to get some more towels?"

She looked at me and I closed my eyes. I was feeling terrible! The man said yes and then she went away. He told me just to lay still and be quiet. Then the woman come back and put a cold towel on my head. It was still hurting bad, like pounding, and my eyes was burning. The lady brought me some milk, and the moment I drank that I threw it up, but the man caught it in the towel so it didn't go over the rug. I felt really bad and I told the man I had to go to the bathroom, and he helped me up and took me over to the bathroom.

In the bathroom I looked in the tub and my shirt was laying there and it was all wet. It was the first time I saw that I didn't have a shirt on, and I saw that there was some mess on the shirt, too. I must have thrown up before. Anyway, I threw up some more and then I washed my face and come out. I didn't know what to do about the shirt and I couldn't think of nothing, either.

When I got out of the bathroom the man asked me if I wanted to try to eat something. I said no. I didn't want to do anything but go to sleep.

"Remember how you got here?" he asked.

"No."

"Well, I had to carry you," he said. "You was in pretty bad shape."

I didn't know what to say so I didn't say nothing.

"My name's Roland," he said. He held his hand out and I reached out to shake it. "You must have drank a lot of whatever it was you was drinking."

"I guess so."

"What's your name?" He sat on the sofa and

folded his hands in his lap.

"Tippy."

"How you feeling now?"

"Okay." I wasn't really feeling okay, I was feeling terrible, but I didn't want to say that. I was thinking about how I was going to get my shirt clean and dry.

"Look, Tippy, you mind if I tell you a story?"

"A story?"

"Yeah, a little story about me?"

"I don't care," I said. I hoped it didn't sound wrong the way I said it, because I didn't mean it to be mean or anything.

"Well, when I was a youngster, about your age"—Mr. Roland crossed his leg—"I was pretty much on my own. Except I had a big brother who lived with me and my aunt. When my aunt passed away, me and Jim used to live together and we used to hustle up our pennies to pay for our room. We used to live in a little place called Harrisburg. Anyway, we used to do little odd jobs after school and whatever work we could find on weekends just so we didn't have to go live in the county home. I had heard bad things about the county home and I figured I didn't want to live there. Neither did Jim. Anyway, I kind of know what it's like to be your age and have problems, see? I figured when I saw you laying out in the street that you must have some kind of problems.

"People don't do things to hurt themselves unless they got problems. And that drinking ain't doing nothing but hurting you. You know that, don't you?"

I shrugged and didn't say nothing.

"Well, I don't want to give you no long lectures or anything. I just want you to know one thing, that if you feel like talking to somebody you can always come on over here and talk to me. Even if you need a little pocket change or something. You know what I mean?"

"Yes."

"Where you live?"

"Over on St. Nicholas."

"I'll take you home."

"No, that's okay," I said. I didn't want Lonnie to see him bringing me home.

"Well, all right, Tippy," he said. "You just remember that when things get a little rough you can always come on over and talk to me. If I ain't home Edna's home."

"It sure beats getting yourself all sick," Edna said. I saw that she had a few little hairs coming out from her chin. She gave me a shirt to wear and she said I could have it. It fit just about fine, too.

"Anyway, I'm going to write down my address on a piece of paper and you just carry it with you or put it someplace safe, okay?"

"Okay."

Mr. Roland seemed nice, and I was really ashamed that he found me in the street like he did.

On the way out I saw one of those things you carry lemonade in. It was on the floor near some sneakers and other stuff, and I thought maybe they was going to go on that bus but didn't.

"You was going on a picnic?" I asked.

"I'm so glad we didn't have to go on that crazy picnic I don't know what to do with myself," Mr. Roland said. "Ain't you, Edna?"

"I sure am," she said. "If we go on another picnic we gonna have to take old Tippy along so we can have a little fun."

I said good-bye and left. I got out to the hallway and Edna, Mr. Roland's wife, came after me. I had forgot to take the paper with their address and name on it. She told me to take good care of myself.

The name on the paper read Roland Sylvester.

It was still pretty early in the afternoon, and I went home and got in bed. My head was still hurting something terrible. When Lonnie got home I was in the bathroom. I thought I was going to throw up again but I didn't. He had that same woman with him from the night before, and he said why didn't I go outside. I told him I didn't feel good, but then he caught an attitude and started hollering so I said okay and left. I went down to the corner and just stood, leaning on a light pole, when this guy come up. It was Mr. Roland again.

"Hey, Tippy, how you doing?" he said. He had a bag like he was coming from the grocery store. He was wearing a bus driver's uniform, too.

"Okay."

"Busy?"

I said I was a little busy even though I wasn't. Then he asked me if I wanted to go ride the bus with him, and I said okay. We went in his car up to Amsterdam Avenue and 129th Street, and he took me into where they kept all the buses. First we went into the office and he signed in. There was a lot of other guys there, too, most of them with bus drivers' uniforms on. They started kidding around with him and they talked about the ball game and that was nice. I don't exactly know why it was nice, maybe because they was calm and friendly. Also because they wanted each other to be talking, too.

We rode around for two hours. I sat right behind Mr. Roland and watched people get on and pay their fare. Then when we got to the end of the line we stopped for coffee and pie and then he put me on another bus and told me to go home. He said I could ride with him whenever I wanted to, and I said that I didn't think I wanted to ride any more.

I liked riding that bus. I had went all the way downtown and saw a lot of things that I hadn't seen before. I had been downtown with Frank, but we was always doing things that you had to look out for, which made me very nervous. I didn't think I had to look out for nothing with me sitting right behind Mr. Roland in the bus. I liked Mr. Roland, too, but I knew if he knew about the grocery store and all them rings and watches and things that he would be upset and wouldn't want me to ride anyway. I didn't blame him.

The thing I noticed mostly was when we was passing Central Park and saw a lot of people playing softball. They was men and women, mostly white, and they didn't have on no regular uniforms, but like T-shirts. And I couldn't see them close up, but I thought they must have been having a good time and liking the way they was. If there was anything I wanted to be, I mean right then, it was them people playing softball in the park. I could ride right by them in the bus and they wouldn't even look up to see me. And if I was walking around in the park, maybe watching the ball game or something, then they would still go on and play.

I thought about them as the bus went on further downtown, thinking about how they was happy, or maybe just looking happy. It was like they was in the real world and I was outside the real world looking at them, because most of the things I wanted to do and wanted to be was like them, happy and doing something with a lot of other people. It was good doing things that everybody else was doing if it was a right thing to do. That was because you had fun doing it and because you was a part of the world you always heard about or maybe saw on television. I thought that those people playing softball liked themselves a lot.

I got home and Lonnie ask me where I been. The lady was gone. I said I went on a bus ride and he said that he used to go on bus rides when he was my age. He had some fried chicken and stuff and we sat down and ate it.

"I used to go over to the bus terminal and get transfers out of the garbage," Lonnie said. "Then I would take the bus for three blocks and get off because it wasn't going in my way except for them three blocks. Sometimes I would wait for a half hour or a hour before I'd have a chance to sneak in the terminal and get a transfer just to go them three blocks. They used to have this old man who used to sit by the door, and his job was to keep people out, I guess.

"Soon as he would see us he would get a broom and start chasing us. Then soon as he would chase one of us the others would run in and get about two or three transfers out of the garbage and we'd be home free."

I didn't say nothing but just sat trying to imagine Lonnie sneaking in and taking the transfers. I couldn't imagine him being little, only just as big as he was, and I couldn't imagine nobody chasing him with a broom, either.

"What you thinking, man?" Lonnie said that with his tough voice.

"Nothing."

"What you mean, *nothing*?" he said. "You got to be thinking *something*."

"I was thinking about what you said," I said.

"I guess you thinking about Carrie." Lonnie threw his last piece of chicken across the room to a bag of garbage under the sink. Two points!

"No."

"Well, ain't no use to thinking about her." He got up and went over and laid on the bed. "She's probably gonna die anyway."

I figured he must have been drinking. Soon as he has even one or two drinks he starts being mean. He laid on the bed and looked at me and I just waited until I finished my chicken and then started for my room.

"What is it, you don't like it here or something?"

"I didn't say that."

"Well, what the hell's the matter with you?" Lonnie sat up on one elbow, and I hoped he wouldn't start hitting on me again.

"Nothing's the matter."

"Then why you acting like you acting?"

"I just wish we could live different, I guess," I said.

"Like how?"

"I don't know. Maybe if we didn't have that stuff before."

"What stuff? You mean them watches and things?"

I nodded.

"Well, let me tell you, sucker." He got up and came over where I was standing. "When I gave you the money from them watches you sure didn't give it back. You and Carrie so damn holy you got angel wings growing out your asses! Here!"

He reached into his pocket and pulled out a

ring. He put it on the table and then he went and laid back down on the bed.

"Now, I'm going to leave that ring right there. Now since you against me, you can go down to the station house and tell the man to come up here and bust me on a possession rap. Then I can have my head beat and go on to jail and you can run to church and thank God that I ain't jiving up your life."

He stayed on the bed and looked at me, and I went on in my room and went to bed. I didn't take my clothes off in case he started in hitting me or something. I heard him go out and I tried to go to sleep but I couldn't. I started thinking about Frank again, only we wasn't ballplayers this time but we just lived together. When I was thinking about Frank I was feeling sorry for myself, and I knew I was, only I didn't care. I just kept on thinking about Frank and me. I thought maybe I would take another name, too. I would call myself Doc, or the Shadow. Then everywhere me and Frank went we would put our names up—Motown and the Shadow.

I thought about going out to get some drinks, but I know I couldn't drink one because my stomach was too upset. Whenever Lonnie started yelling at me my stomach would get upset. Then I couldn't drink anything that was too sweet. I could probably drink a chocolate drink, I thought, but I really didn't feel like going outside. I got up and went out to the bathroom. I saw that Lonnie had left some of his drink in the bottle, it was almost half full. I poured a little in a glass and took it into my room. It was terrible—I didn't see how he could drink it. I went back out and looked in the refrigerator and found some orange soda and put it in that. It wasn't too bad that way, and I fell asleep.

When I woke up I had a headache again. I heard voices, and when I went out Lonnie had that lady up again. He didn't say nothing but she said hello. I didn't want to say hello to her, but I knew if I didn't Lonnie would be on my case, so I did. She left after a while to go to work. Lonnie asked me if I wanted to eat breakfast with him and I started to say no, but then I saw he had his attitude on so I said okay. We went down to 125th Street to eat at McDonald's.

"So what you want me to do?" Lonnie said as we walked up St. Nicholas.

"What you mean?" I asked.

"You want me to get a job and go square, right?" he said.

That sounded okay to me and I said so.

"Then I got to do it," he said.

He used to say things like that all the time. Things that made you say something back. The longer it took him to say what was really happening the worse it always was. I figured this was not going to be good because when I asked him what it was he had to do he just said, "You know." Then when I said I didn't know, he said, "You don't know?"

"No, I don't know."

We had reached the stoop and it was empty and we sat on it. Lonnie sat for a long time, looking down like he was sad or something. The numbers man came around and Lonnie put in 065 and combinated it. He also played a 0 lead. Clyde Johnson came by and said he was on his way to Betsy Head Pool and to tell his brother if I saw him.

"I got to get me a stake," Lonnie said.

"For supper?"

"No, a stake to get started with in this 'new life' you got planned for me," he said.

"Oh, how you going to do that?" I asked.

"I don't know," he said. "You got any ideas?"

"I know a guy who works in the bus company," I told him. "Maybe he could get you a job driving a bus or something."

"You know a guy that can get me a job?" He

looked at me. "You sound like some of them whiteys downtown. Where you know this cat from, anyway?"

"I met him a couple of days ago and he let me ride around on his bus."

"He a faggot?"

"No."

"How you know?"

I didn't say anything more, and he asked me again, and I told him I didn't know for sure, but he was married. Lonnie said that didn't mean nothing, a lot of freaks was married.

"You stay away from this guy," Lonnie said. "I don't want my son around no faggots. A lot of faggots figure they can turn you before your manhood gets set, then you messed up for life."

"Okay."

"Yeah. You ain't been around long enough to know that kind of stuff," he said. "And anyway, how come he messing with you? He can't make no children of his own?"

"I don't know," I said. "I thought he was just being okay."

"Yeah, uh-huh." Lonnie looked down his nose at me. "A lot of cats can't make no children of their own so they try to get next to another guy's kids and then chump him off by being nice. I dug that action before. People look at you and start asking you why you ain't got no kids, but if they see you with a kid all the time, especially a boy kid, then they think you a man."

Then he didn't say nothing for a while, and I figured he would get up and say, "Later," like he usually did when he didn't have anything to say, but he didn't.

"I been thinking about what I'm doing, too," he said. "And I figure that maybe I could open up a small business, a candy store or something, or either get some money and take a training course in something like refrigeration or that other thing they had on television the other night."

"Welding."

"Yeah. A trade. But to do that I got to get a stake. Now, what you say about that?"

"About what?"

"What I'm talking, African or some jive?"

"It's okay."

"See, I figure if I can get a heavy taste, just one time, I can sit back and see what I really want to do instead of setting around while the welfare takes away all your energy. Because that's what happens, you know. You get on welfare and then you don't want to do nothing because as soon as you start something the welfare cuts your ass off!

See what I mean?"

"Yes." I said it but I really didn't see it.

"So if I get this heavy taste and then get a trade, everything'll be cool?"

"Yeah," I said. But my heart wasn't in it.

He was talking about stealing again, and I was saying it was okay. I thought about it for a while on purpose when it didn't leave my mind, and I decided that maybe it was all right. If he could steal something and not get into trouble and then go straight it would be cool. But if he was gonna keep on stealing, then it wouldn't be cool at all because I was getting to the point I couldn't stand it.

It wasn't even the stealing part that was so bad. I mean, I didn't like him stealing, and that's the part that was wrong and everything. But the real bad part, the really bad part, was I was getting not to like him. He was beginning to look like something bad to me, like a mangy dog or something. No, not like a mangy dog because a mangy dog was bad because of the way he looked and Lonnie really looked okay on the outside. But when I looked at him I wanted to see something more than just Lonnie who did what he did. I wanted to see somebody great who looked like he was proud of himself and everything, the same way that I wanted to see me when I looked in the mirror. When I looked at me in the mirror I used to see some of Lonnie in me, the way I looked. Especially around the nose because me and him had just about the same nose. I think we had the same kind of legs, too—big on the top and little on the bottom.

But I wanted to see Lonnie looking special, and I wanted it so bad that sometimes I would think about it for a long time. One time I daydreamt about him winning a lot of money on a number. Then I switched it to the lottery so he could get on television. Then they would come to the house, and me and him would stand in front of the stoop, and they would talk to him, and I would sit on the steps. Maybe I would hold the basketball.

We sat around and talked some more, and then he said he had to go downtown and he gave me three dollars. I sat on the stoop for a long time. I started thinking about what I had said and then pushed it out of my mind. I didn't want to think about it at all.

10

I didn't have nothing to do so I went over to see Denise. I was thinking about going downtown and look for Frank but I didn't think I could find him. I thought Denise would be home and I bought two bottles of Dr Pepper and took them to her place.

"Hi, Tippy." She said it so low I could hardly hear her, and I figured she was sad. She was sad a lot, I thought, even when nothing too bad was happening to her. When she was with Bubba she was kind of happy, but then he would get to talking to Lonnie and Stone and either drinking or smoking herb and Denise would just sit around and wait until Bubba told her to go home.

I opened the Dr Peppers and we sat around and watched television for a while. Denise's television was old and the picture was always fuzzy. The only thing that helped a little was if you hung a wire coat hanger from the antenna or if you stood about two feet away from it, on the right side.

"Guess what?" Denise looked over at me.

"What?"

"I'm gonna have a baby." She looked over at me like she wanted to see what I thought about it. Then she looked away.

Almost everything in Denise's place was green. The walls was light green and the drapes was dark green with pictures of swans on them. One time when I was at her house I drew the swans from the drapes and she made a big deal of it.

"Bubba gonna be the father," Denise said.

"You glad?"

"I don't know." She was wearing dungarees and she got up and pulled the pants legs down a little and then sat back down. "Sometimes I'm glad and sometimes I'm not glad."

"Is Bubba glad?"

"He's glad," Denise said, "but he don't want to get married."

"How come?"

"He said if we get married then he'll get tied down and everything. He said he'll give the baby his name, though."

"Bubba?"

"No, Vann, that's his last name."

"You want to get married?"

She didn't say nothing and I figured she did. I had heard a lot about people having babies and things and getting on welfare. I asked her when she was going to the hospital.

"I might not even go," she said. "Sometimes they have the baby at home with the father."

"In the house?"

"Yeah," she said. "You wanna come?"

"No."

"Why not, then you can practice on being a father," she said, smiling. "Then when you and your old lady have a baby you can just pop it on out!"

"Get out of here." I balled up the bag that the Dr Peppers was in and threw it at her, and she caught it and threw it back at me, except she missed by a lot. "Bubba going to be here when you have it and all?"

"Sure, he the daddy, ain't he? I might have a whole party with all my friends. Then when the baby come out she gonna think this a whole cool world."

"You make too much noise and she might not even come out!"

"She better come out with her fresh tail self," Denise said. "I ain't gonna carry her around in me a whole year."

"Bubba better start saving him some money." I picked the bag off the floor and threw it in the garbage.

"The baby's gonna be on welfare," Denise said.

"How you know? It's not even here yet!"

"'Cause I'm on welfare," Denise answered. "I know it ain't gonna come here with no job!"

"How come you're on welfare?" I asked.

"'Cause I'm something . . ." Denise sat down and screwed her face up like she was trying to think of a word. But I didn't think she was really trying to think it up because her face didn't get screwed up like that when she was trying to think of something.

"You're what?" I asked.

"Oh, yeah, limited."

"What does that mean?"

"I don't know," she said, opening the refrigerator door. "You want something to eat?"

"What you got?"

"Some chicken and some leftover hamburgers that 'bout hard as rocks."

"I'll take the chicken," I said. "What does that mean about you being limited?"

"I don't know," she said again. She was taking the chicken out of the refrigerator. It was in a blue bowl with a plastic cover on it, and she smelled it before she put it in a pot. "Something about not catching on to things too fast."

I knew what she meant because sometimes I didn't think she caught on to things at all, even though she would smile and act like she did. I wanted to ask her some more about it, but I thought maybe I had better not because she might get upset. Anyway we had the chicken, which was chopped up with onion and mustard. It was pretty good. Denise was the only person I knew except Grandma Carrie who could make chicken that I really liked. She even made it better than Grandma Carrie.

"How you know it's gonna be a girl?"

"I know."

"How you know?"

"I know."

"I know, too."

"How?"

"I don't know."

"I know you don't know. You too young."

"That's okay."

"I wouldn't mind getting married," Denise said. "When I found out I was pregnant I dreamed about getting married."

"How'd you find out?"

"I just dreamed it."

"No, about the baby."

"Oh, I miss my month, and whenever I miss it I have to go down to the clinic," she said. "You want some more chicken?"

"Uh-uh."

"You didn't like it."

"I didn't say I didn't like it."

"You'd be a funny husband."

"Why?" I had a mouthful of chicken when I asked her, and I thought that was kind of funny by itself.

"I don't know," Denise said. "Maybe you'd be a nice husband."

"I'd be the serious joint," I said.

"That's what all you men say," Denise answered. "Bubba said that when he gets ready to settle down he'll get married and then he'll be a good husband, but if he gets married too soon, then he won't be a good husband 'cause his nature is too high."

"What does that mean?"

"That he has to fool around with a lot of girls."

"Oh."

"When I get married I'm gonna have a practice wedding first, like they do on television, just to check everything out. Then I'm gonna have my niece—you know little Darlene?"

"Real light skin and kind of fat?"

"She ain't fat."

"She ain't skinny, either."

"Yeah, her, anyway, she's gonna be my flower girl."

"You think Bubba is ever gonna marry you?"

"I don't know. I don't even care if I don't get married," she said. She finished up the chicken on her plate and then took her plate and mine and started washing them in the sink. The soap made bubbles that covered her hands as she washed the dishes and the pan and then the sink. She put everything away, and in a minute it looked as if we had never even eaten. I picked the Dr Pepper bottles off the table and put them in the garbage.

"You want to get married?" she asked me.

"Who? Me?"

"Yeah."

"No."

"How come?"

"I'm not old enough."

"You old enough to have a practice marriage," she said. "C'mon, you want to have a practice marriage?"

"That's silly!"

"You ain't nothing but silly yourself!" she said, getting up and taking my hand. "C'mon, it won't hurt you."

I stood up and she got a little bench she had with a plant on it and put it in front of the window. The plant was right in the middle but she put it to one side. Then she got a Bible, a real one, out and put it on the bench. It was getting real silly, and I sat back down, and she pulled me back up again.

"C'mon, it ain't gonna kill you," she said. "Now you stand over there, and when the music start we come over here, and then we walk up to the bench."

She had this big smile on her face and then she started humming the tune they always play when people get married and walking towards the center where we was supposed to turn. I started walking, too, just the way she did, which was one step and then bring your feet together and then another step and do the same thing. When we got to the middle we turned and walked up to the bench and then she kneeled down. I didn't want to kneel down, but she gave me a little punch like we was really in church or something and she didn't want nobody to know that I was messing up, so I kneeled down.

Then she took my hand and put it on the Bible, and she put her hand on mine, and then I really wanted to stop because I didn't like messing around with the Bible. But she was really looking serious. She had this real calm look and she was holding herself up funny, not funny, but like a knight in shining armor or something like that.

"Do you, Tippy, take Denise Lawton for your wife?"

I didn't say nothing, but then she gave a poke and I said, "I do."

"Do you, Denise Lawton, take Tippy for your husband?" she asked herself, and then she said that she did. Then she pronounced us man and wife and kissed me. Right on the mouth.

"See," she said, "it didn't hurt, did it?"

It didn't hurt, but it was different, because I felt different inside. I knew that what we had done was important to Denise, and I felt sorry for her in a way and close to her in a way. We was quiet for a while and Denise put the radio on and asked me if I wanted to dance, only I couldn't dance, and so she just sat next to me and leaned against me and I held her hand. After a long while I said I thought I better go and she said okay, and before I left she kissed me again, on the cheek this time but it was close to being the same as when she kissed me on the mouth.

On the way home I hoped that God didn't think I was really married to Denise, and if He wondered about having my hand on the Bible and all and saying how I took her to be my wife, it was because Denise wanted it like that and maybe even needed it. I also wondered if God would see it the same as me, or if anybody would.

◇　◇　◇

Denise made me think of birds, even though I really can't stand birds because once Grandma Carrie had a bird and its name was Gregory, just like a person. Well, one morning Grandma Carrie went to work and I got up late and made breakfast for myself. The breakfast was cornflakes and I thought that I would give some to Gregory. I took the cornflakes in to Gregory, and I didn't see him sitting in his cage. Once before he had got sick and Grandma Carrie took him to the animals hospital and they gave her something to put on him. I thought maybe he was sick again and I went to the telephone to see if Grandma Carrie had left a number I could call her at so I could ask if she took the bird to the hospital. He was a snow-white canary and about one year old.

There was no number so I figured that Grandma Carrie must have been on a new job. I was getting ready to go outside when I heard a little cheep and I thought that maybe he got out of the cage and got stuck behind something. I went back in where we kept him and couldn't see him around the room and then I looked in the cage again and he was laying on the bottom. He was breathing heavy. I didn't know what to do so I waited around for a while to see if Grandma Carrie would call and give me her number. She didn't call and so I took Gregory out of his cage and went over to the animals hospital on Manhattan Avenue. By the time I got over there he was dead. The guy at the hospital said that birds died easily because they was so weak to begin with.

Denise was like a weak bird. Sometimes I wanted to go over and talk to her because I didn't have nobody else to talk to, and at the same time I didn't want to because I didn't want to see her like she was. I really didn't like to see things that was hurt easy.

I buried Gregory in Morningside Park. I couldn't find a box so I buried him in Reynolds Wrap.

11

"Yeah, so I was just going along with my man, Billy, 'cause he was looking for a gig," Lonnie said. "And this chick asks me if I want a application— hey, why not?—so I fill it out and now I got to go down there again tomorrow to their doctor and take a physical, and then I got the gig!"

Lonnie was real happy. He had bought some soda and some tuna fish and made sandwiches, and he was putting it out as he talked. It was the first time I had seen him excited. I had seen him happy before, kind of happy, anyway, but not really excited. He was so excited it made me excited, too.

"What you going to be doing?" I asked.

"It's like a trainee job," he said. "I'm supposed to learn how to fix all the machines they have in their different offices. I start at three dollars a hour while I'm training, and then I go up to six dollars a hour in two years. That's some boss bread."

"That's okay."

"Okay? Okay?" Lonnie looked at me with his eyes half shut like they was when he was mad, but he had a smile, or almost a smile, on his face, too. "That ain't okay, that's the serious joint! You start working for some big company like that and you got you a good job for life. You can retire from a job like that!"

We ate the tuna-fish sandwiches and sat around and watched some television, mostly news, until we heard Bubba call from the street. Lonnie looked out the window and said wait a minute, he was coming right down.

"Hey, man, c'mere." Lonnie called me over to where he was changing his shoes. "Look, don't go telling Bubba or Stone or nobody about this gig, see?"

"Okay."

"Ain't that I don't want to turn them on—hand me that towel—"

I handed him the towel and he wiped the dust off his shoes with it.

"It's just I want to see how things go, you know—how the people gonna act."

I said okay, and then Lonnie went downstairs to see Bubba. I looked out the window, and he and Bubba was walking on down the street, and Bubba was walking cool but Lonnie was walking hoppy, like he was still excited. I didn't know what to do so I watched television for a while longer. Then I decided to go over to see Grandma Carrie.

When I got to the hospital, the nurse said that there was only twenty more minutes to visiting hour. I said okay and thought that it was good because then I could leave and she wouldn't be upset or nothing.

It took her ten minutes to come downstairs and the first thing she asked me was how come I didn't come to see her no more. I didn't know what to say so I didn't say nothing, just put my head down.

"Out of sight, out of mind," she said. "I guess you hoping that Carrie gets carried out of here soon, huh?"

"No."

"That was sure a weak no," she said.

I was sorry that I hadn't went and saw her more, but I hadn't been thinking about nothing except what I was doing. I put my arm around her, and when I did that she started to cry, and I held her for a while until she stopped. I held her even when it was past the visiting hour and the nurse came down. The nurse looked at me and looked at the clock, and then she did little things until she had to come over and take Grandma Carrie back upstairs. She told me to wait downstairs for her, and I did.

When I was waiting I thought about how I had been with Grandma Carrie and with Denise and how they was something like each other. Only I didn't like thinking about it because I didn't know what I could do about Denise or Grandma Carrie. A lot of things I couldn't do nothing about I didn't like to think about.

"How you doing?" The nurse sat down next to me.

"Okay."

"Your grandmother gets real worried when you don't come and see her, you know."

"I know."

"She said you living with your father."

"Uh-huh."

"Everything working out okay?"

"Yeah."

"You come around and visit her more. People get old like that they get to be like children and they need somebody to come around and visit with them. And if you need anything you just ask me. Don't be shamefaced now."

"I'm not shamed."

"Tippy's your name, right?"

"Yes."

"Well, my name is Miss Willens. You need anything you just ask for me. Now you go on home before it gets dark."

Miss Willens was nice. I was glad that she was taking care of Grandma Carrie, and it made me feel good that she was worried about me. I didn't want nothing from her, but I liked her, and it was nice she should say that.

When I got home Lonnie was already there watching television. He had bought some real chicken instead of the already cooked chicken, and he was cooking it on the stove. It smelled good when he was making it, but when we went to eat it it wasn't done so we had to put it back on the stove, and then we went to eat it again and it still wasn't done, and he got mad and the last time he put it on the stove it got burned, so we went out and got some hamburgers at McDonald's.

"That chicken didn't come out too good," Lonnie said.

When he said that I couldn't help myself. I just started laughing about as hard as I could. He said the chicken didn't come out too good, and what it really was was just about all burned up. A couple of people in McDonald's turned and looked at me a little, but I was still laughing. After a while I stopped laughing.

"Can you cook chicken?" Lonnie asked me.

"No," I said.

"Then how come you laughing?"

I could see he was getting kind of mad, so I didn't say much but just finished eating the French fries and stuff. He looked at me like he didn't know what to say, and finally I told him I was sorry that I laughed at his chicken.

"It ain't easy to be no damned father, you know," he said. "You got a lot of responsibility and stuff."

"You like being a father?" I asked.

"It's okay," he said. "If you don't mess it up, then it's okay, but a lot of dudes mess it up, and then they ain't nothing and their kids ain't nothing either. I might get me one of those books about how to raise kids."

He looked at me as if I was supposed to say something, but I didn't know what to say. The only thing I thought of was my friend Dean, who had bought a hamster, and me and him went to the pet shop and got a book on how to raise hamsters. I could just see Lonnie going into that pet shop and asking for a book about how to raise me. I started laughing again, and he thought I was laughing about his chicken like I was before, and he got up and walked out. I had to hurry up to catch up with him. He acted like he was embarrassed, and on the way home he said he could really make some good pork chops. For some reason I started laughing at that, too, and he said I didn't have no sense at all.

Then he asked me if I wanted to hear a joke, and I said okay.

He said this guy was in prison and they was going to put him in the electric chair. He was real scared and crying, and another guy said not to be worried. He said going to the electric chair was just like going to work. Just don't sit down on the job, he said.

Well, I started laughing at that until I almost fell down, and he was laughing, too. We laughed and fooled around all the way until we got home.

"You're all right," he said.

"I'm all right when you're all right," I said. I was sorry I said it, thinking that maybe he would get mad, but he didn't. He just smiled.

"You think I'm hard on you, don't you?" he asked.

"No," I said, hoping that I said it soft enough for God not to hear.

"Well, if I'm hard on you it's just because I want you to be something when you grow up."

"What did you want to be when you were little?" I asked.

"What did I want to be?"

"Yeah."

"You ain't even gonna believe it," he said.

"Yes, I will," I said.

"I wanted to be the King of England!"

"The what?"

"Yeah, I saw where the Queen over there made some guy a knight, see? And what he did was to play some sport. Maybe he climbed a mountain or something. So I figured I was going to be a basketball player and then she was gonna make me a knight. Then when she made me a knight I would just work my way on up to being king. I even had me a queen picked out. This little white girl was in the third grade with me. She was going to be the queen and I was gonna be the king, see. Then I told my father and he laugh and say I couldn't be no king. Then I got suspended about a month later—"

"For what?"

"I cursed at a teacher. Then I got suspended and they put me off the basketball team. So I went and told this girl—her name was Sara Upton—never will forget that girl—that she might have to wait for a while.

"I got about your age, maybe a little older, I was in so much trouble I left school. I didn't exactly leave. I just got into trouble one time, and they told me I couldn't come back unless I brought my father to school or my mother. I told my father and he said he didn't have no time to be running around to the school every time he turned around. So I just stopped going."

"You ever see that girl?"

"The queen? Yeah, I saw her with her husband in a store downtown. She was still pretty."

"Was you mad at your father 'cause he didn't go to school?" I asked.

He looked at me but he didn't say nothing, and I figured I'd better not ask again.

12

They had the Catholic relays on the block the next day, and I watched part of them from the stoop. They had some nuns there, and I saw one of the boys who had chased me that day from the church. He saw me, too.

"You live around here?" he said.

"Yeah, I live around here, so what?"

"Nothing, I just asked," he said. "Father Morrow said he wondered where you was."

"So?"

"So nothing," he said. "The only reason we chased you that day is because Father Morrow told us to follow you. We thought you had taken something, but then he said he just wanted somebody else to talk to you."

I didn't believe him, but he looked kind of scared so I didn't do nothing. I just watched the relays. They was the kind where you ran against people your own age and the winner got little plastic trophies. Denise was there and she asked me if

I was going to run, and I said I didn't think so. One lady, a nun, asked me if I wanted to run, and I said okay, mostly because Denise was there, I think.

I had to run with three other boys. I was the third one to run. There was three teams. We had to run from one sewer to the other and give the other guy a stick. Then the other guy would run the other way back to the first sewer with the stick. On the first sewer my team was last. On the second sewer we was still last, and then it was my turn. I got the stick and I cut out and I ran past the other guys on other teams, but then I started getting tired and they started catching up with me. I put all I had into it, but they still beat me, but just by a little bit. I gave our last guy the stick and then I almost threw up. Everybody was yelling and cheering, and when I turned around the guy from my team was way out front. We won and then we got a trophy, and they said we could run against the older boys if we wanted to for the block championship relay team.

The guy who had run last on our team said to me that if I could catch up with the guys or even come close, then he would have a chance to beat them. I was nervous, really nervous.

There was only two teams, us and the older guys. It was the last race of the day, and most of the trophies was gone. I had one that Denise was holding, and I couldn't wait for the day to end and Lonnie come home and see it.

Our first guy got beat by a lot, and our second guy wasn't doing too good either.

"I'm gonna run your ass raggedy, man," their third guy said. I saw him around the block a lot—he used to take money from some of the small kids. "And I'm gonna kick your ass if you even come close to me."

I didn't even pay him no mind. I knew I couldn't beat him 'cause I saw him fight and he was good, but I wasn't going to lose just because I was scared.

He got the stick before me and started running. He was running like he was cool, and I didn't know how I should run. I remembered getting real tired the last time and thought about taking it easy on the first part, but then I started getting tired right away and figured I might as well run fast as I could right away. I started catching up and everybody started yelling, and he turned around to look at me, and then he started to really run hard, but he fell down. I got my stick over to our last man, and he could have just walked because that guy was just laying there. We won and we got the last medal. When we was waiting to get the trophy the guy I ran against came over and stood close to me and said he was going to punch me in my mouth.

"You're going to try," I said. My heart was beating fast.

Then he just looked at me and said I wasn't even worth getting his hands dirty, and then he walked away. Then they called me to come and get the trophy, and I was hoping that I could remember to think about him saying that to me and what I said to him, because I think that whatever it was that exactly happened, I won.

Lonnie wasn't home when I got there, so I just sat around and waited. While I waited I imagined running in a hundred races and winning them all. Then I imagined running in the Olympics and I won that, too. I could see myself watching me on television getting the medal put around my neck. It was such a good feeling that I almost cried, even though it was all imaginary. Frank was in some of the dreams but only when we was together on a relay team. I didn't want him beating me and I didn't want to beat him, either.

I thought about Denise seeing the race and was just about to go over to her house when Lonnie came home. He looked tired and I wasn't going to show him the trophies right away but he saw them sitting on the table.

"Where they come from?" he said.

"They had some races in the street and they gave

out prizes to the winners and I won them."

"No lie?"

"No lie!"

"Hey, man." He lifted his hand up and I put out my palm and he slapped it. "That's all right."

"Thanks."

"Really, I really mean that," he said. "That's really all right."

He gave me five again and then he sat down and looked at the trophies. He held them in his hands, and they didn't look too big, but he kept looking at them. It made me feel real good to see him look at the trophies because I could see he was happy about them. It was the first time I felt like a son and all.

"You know I never got a trophy?" he said.

"No?"

"No, man." Lonnie put the trophies down side by side. "That's one of the reasons why I'm glad you got some. I played basketball, ran track, and everything and never got a damn trophy. We was supposed to get trophies one year when Marty's, over on a Hundred-twenty-fifth Street, sponsored us. We came in third in this tournament—"

"Basketball?"

"Yeah. We came in third behind a team from Morningside Community Center and another team from Milbank. Then they found out about a guy we had on the team named Junior who was overage. That guy only played in one game and he didn't do nothing in that game. Then they gave our trophies to the fourth-place team and put us last. Ain't that a bitch?"

"Yeah."

Stone came by a little later with a white girl and asked Lonnie if he wanted to go down to The Spot—The Spot was a bar they used to hang out in sometime—and Lonnie said no. When Stone left, me and Lonnie watched television until it was time to go to bed.

Lonnie woke me up the next day and asked me if I could get by on just a dollar because he was kind of short. I told him I still had money from before, almost four dollars, and he could have that if he needed it. He said no, it was okay, and he left for work.

I thought about Lonnie a lot that day. I was glad to see him happy and I was thinking that maybe he wasn't going to steal any more. I remembered what Grandma Carrie had said about a Christian not being able to stand no thief. I figured God would be as glad as me if Lonnie stopped stealing things, and so would the people he was stealing from. I was sure that he wouldn't steal any more and would maybe just have to stay in hell for a little while. I thought about me and him going to this place after we died and this guy with a long beard and all saying what our sins was and me and him just standing there in robes. Then they would say that I could go straight to heaven and Lonnie would have to go to hell for a while and burn. Then I would say that I would go with him and burn for the same time he had to put in and then we could go to heaven together. Then I thought about burning some more and figured I'd wait for him.

I had another good day doing nothing, mostly because I didn't want to spend the money in case Lonnie needed it. I took a walk in the park and I saw Pedro and he was drinking. He asked me if I wanted a drink, and I said okay without even thinking about it. It was strawberry, and he had put some ice cream in it and it was really good. I remembered what had happened before when I had drank too much, and I only had one drink.

That was funny about drinking. Most of the time, if something hurt me or made me sick, then I wouldn't do it any more if I could help it. But when I drank too much and felt bad, then it was like it was part of what I was doing. Because I felt bad, real bad, and wanted everyone to know that I did.

Sometimes I would imagine going over to see Denise and having her take care of me when I was sick. But even if I was by myself it was something more real when you was sick from whiskey than when you was feeling bad because you didn't like the way you was.

I couldn't get them trophies off my mind. I thought about putting them in a bag and taking them downtown to see if I could find Frank and show them to him, but I didn't. I figured I wouldn't find him again, and even if I did he might think I was showing off or something. I wanted to show them to somebody else and tried to think of somebody. Grandma Carrie was out because she probably wouldn't understand what they were for. Also, I figured since she was the one in the hospital I should pay attention to her instead of bringing my things in so she can pay attention to me. The only other people I could think of was the Johnson brothers, Mr. Roland, and Denise. And Denise had already seen them once.

I couldn't find the Johnson brothers, so I put the trophies in a bag and took them to Mr. Roland's house.

He asked me if I had won the trophies and I said yes, that I did.

"Hey, that's okay, these are really nice," he said.

"Ain't they nice, honey?"

"Very nice," his wife said. I looked over to where she was standing, looking through some papers, and I saw she hadn't even hardly seen the trophies.

"You know, something like this means two things, Tippy," Mr. Roland said, putting on kind of an official voice. "The first thing it means is that you won something and you should be real proud of it. You did what you did best, and that's something to be proud of. And the next thing it means is that you can do other things the same way. You know what I'm talking about?"

"Uh-huh. I can do good in school and things like that."

"Right. That's exactly what it means, and that's what I would like you to do. Everything you do you say to yourself, 'I'm going to get a trophy for this.'" Mr. Roland put the trophy down on the table and crossed his leg. His legs were stubby, and he had to hold the one on top across the other so it wouldn't slide off. "Even if you know there's no trophy you have to try as if there is one. Because the real trophy is what you accomplish."

He went on for a while and I was feeling good, but then I wished it was Lonnie that was saying it and not him. I always felt better if the people who are supposed to say something say it. Like if you do okay in school it's better if the teacher says it. And if you do something okay outside of school, then it's cool if your father says it and not the teacher. It was kind of like I wanted a special place for me to be where I would be as special as the place. So even though I dug Mr. Roland saying good things about the trophies, it wasn't as good as when Lonnie said them.

When I got home Lonnie was there. I took the trophies into my room because I didn't want him to know I was carrying them around and showing them to everybody. When I came out of the room he was sitting in the same place he was when I went in and I could see something was the matter.

I didn't say nothing for a while and he didn't say nothing. I saw there was some whiskey on the bureau and I knew he had been drinking. He was sitting on the windowsill, looking down on the street, and every once in a while you could see a color on his face from when a big truck passed. He didn't look mad or nothing, just sad. I asked him if he wanted me to make anything to eat. He didn't say nothing for a while, and then he said no.

"I don't have no appetite."

"Something wrong?"

"Lost the damn job."

"How come?"

"I don't know," he said. He took a deep breath and then he let it all out again until his shoulders drooped. There was a pencil on the table, and I sat there and started drawing him, not looking at him like a regular artist, but just drawing him without making him feel self-conscious. He looked over at me once or twice to see what I was doing, and then he asked me, and I said I was drawing him, and he said not to be doing that, so I stopped. He got up and made a drink for himself with the whiskey and some Dr Pepper, and I asked him could I have a drink. He looked at me and I looked back at him, and then he put the bottle on the table not too far away from me instead of on the bureau, and so I picked it up and made a drink, too. He looked at me doing it and he didn't say nothing, but he didn't look happy about it either, so after I made the drink I just left it there on the table.

"The check from the welfare came today," I said. I remembered that I had brought it upstairs and thought maybe it would make him feel better.

"I go in this morning and the girl who works for the boss says he wants to see me," Lonnie said. "So I go in to see him and he says that I should work on the duplicator. So I go into the duplicator room to see what was wrong with it and one of the other guys, the salesman, said that the paper wasn't coming through. So I look at it and I see the paper is all bunched up under that aluminum part, the drum. This salesman seem like he okay, and he's standing looking to see what I'm doing, but what happened, I picked up the duplicator and turned it on the side to get at the paper, and the fluid come out and get all over him, and he starts cursing me out and shit. So I told him he shouldn't have been standing on top of me and it wouldn't have happened. I mean, he was standing right on top of me.

"Then he went out and started talking to the boss's secretary and talking about how I'm stupid and whatnot. So I told him he was the one that was stupid for standing so near the damn thing. Me and him got into a argument and he starts calling me names and I call him names right back and first thing you know I ain't got a job."

"What you going to do?"

"I don't know," he said.

Lonnie took another drink and finished it real quick. I felt sorry for him because he really acted like he wanted the job. He drank up the rest of the whiskey and then he went out and bought some more with the money from the welfare check. He got drunk and fell asleep, and the woman that stayed with him sometime came by, but we couldn't wake him up. She said that she was going to invite him over to dinner, and then she asked me if I wanted to come over and pick up some food for him so he could eat it when he woke up. I said okay.

I went over to Peggy's house—that's what her name was—and she wrapped up some food in Reynolds paper. Then she started telling me about how she was in love with Lonnie and she could adopt me if she and Lonnie got married. She asked me if I would like that, and I said yes, but I really didn't mean it because I couldn't see her being my mother.

Lonnie didn't wake up any more that night, and so I told him about the food in the morning and told him what Peggy had said. He said Peggy was stupid and always wanted to get married. I asked Lonnie if he was going to marry her and he said no.

"I married your mama and that was enough," he said. "Your Grandma Carrie didn't want me to marry her. She thought I wasn't good enough for her sweet daughter. That was one sweet chickie, man." Lonnie unwrapped the food that Peggy had sent over, looked at it, then wrapped it up again and threw it into the garbage bag. "Sometimes she used to play hooky from school and me and her would go for a ride on the Circle Line pretending like we was going to Europe or something. She used to make up all these wild-ass stories, and I would sit there and listen to them. She had my nose wide open. Have me do stupid stuff, you know, like holding hands and walking through leaves. She used to be big on that walking-through-the-leaves number. When it would get about November or early December, just before Christmas, she would say, 'Let's go for a walk,' and then you know you got to walk out in the leaves. She'd be going on about how pretty they was, and I could really dig where she was coming from.

"Then when she died your grandma kind of blamed it on me. Like I caused it or something. The doctor said she had a hemorrhage. Your mama was okay, really. I mean she was okay. When I first met your mama she was Miss Lady, you know what I mean? And I was just me, just Lonnie. Then I was going to do all these things and be all these things just to please her. I don't think I could do all them things anyway. She knowed it, too. Sure she did. She knowed it."

"You sorry she died?"

"What kind of a dumb-ass question is that?"

"Something to say."

"Sure I'm sorry she died," Lonnie said.

"Grandma Carrie said I look like she did."

"Yeah, you look something like her," Lonnie said, looking at me. "You simple like she was, too.

She could find her a little piece of anything and give you ten damn reasons why that little piece was okay. I can't stand no simple woman, and I can't stand no woman going around understanding your ass to death. That's another thing she always done. Understand.

"One time I was working for this truck outfit. Felson Brothers or something like that, and they docked me 'cause I was out from work two days, see. So I knew I had the money to pay the rent and all, but then we wouldn't have nothing to eat. Not much anyway. We had just had a fight about how we never went nowhere since she was pregnant. That was you. So I stop off and get in this crap game that a guy I knew was running. He said he was setting this guy up and I should get in on the game. Well, this guy had big money and I'm watching him real close. Never will forget that sucker because he had hands smaller than a woman's.

"Anyway, I got my eye on this guy and I'm shooting crap. And this guy with the little hands is winning all the damn money. Then they getting ready to break the game up and everybody standing around talking about how we gonna get together next week. So I pulls my man over and say how come he didn't set this guy up. He talking about the guy is all set up for next week. Now all my damn money is gone and I got to go home and look in your mama's face, and I ain't got nothing in my pocket but a story.

"I walked around half the night, doing this and doing that and figuring out something to say. I couldn't think of nothing so I got mad. I finally got home and she was up walking the floor and crying and saying that she thought something had happened to me. I said ain't nothing happened to me except I lost all our damn money in a crap game.

"You know what she said? She said she understand. Now ain't that a blip? What I look like, some kind of child? You ain't supposed to be understanding no *man*. A man is supposed to *do*. You know what I'm talking about? And what you laughing about?"

I was laughing a little because I started to say that I understood. I didn't say nothing, though, and he said I was about the most simple person he ever met.

13

"We all in this together," Bubba said. "We got to chip in. And you the only one that didn't come up with your money."

"I told you I'm gonna have the money tomorrow," Lonnie said. I didn't know where he was going to get the money from, because the welfare check wasn't due for about another week and the old one had just about run out. Anyway, he and Stone and Bubba and another guy they called Danny was talking for about a hour before they left. Denise was there, too, and me and her stayed in my room while they was talking. I heard some of it, about enough to figure out what they was talking about. It was something about a bank, and I thought they was talking about holding it up.

When Bubba and them had left, Lonnie sat around for a while and then he went out and said he would be back later. He only stayed a little while and then he came back and told me to come with him. We went up to a place on 132nd Street and he kept asking me things like was I on his side or not. I said yes, I was.

"What's that mean?" he said.

"It means I am," I said.

"Yeah, well, we'll see."

We sat for a while near the park, and then he told me to come on with him, and we went down the street and into one of the houses. We walked through the hall and out a back door and went down into the backyard of the house, and I started getting nervous. It was dark in the backyard, but I was more nervous because I thought we was going to steal something, and so I said a prayer to God that we wouldn't be stealing anything. We walked around in the dark a little bit, and Lonnie was looking around. Then he went to one door and pushed it but it didn't open. He reached into his pocket and pulled out a big screwdriver and started prying at the door, and finally, after a long time, the door came open. Lonnie listened for a minute and he didn't hear nothing, so he took me by the arm and we went in. He closed the door and it was black inside. My heart was beating and my legs started sweating, and I could feel the sweat running down inside my pants and it was cold. Lonnie lit a match and I could see we was in a room with boxes of stuff like candy and cookies. There was piles of magazines and newspapers, too. Lonnie found some batteries and a flashlight and he got that to working. He went to the other door and turned the flashlight out and opened it up. It was a candy store, and I could see around easy even without the flashlight because the light from outside was coming through the big glass window. Lonnie crouched down and went behind the counter and I went with him. When we was behind the counter he started messing with the cash register and he got it open, but there wasn't nothing in it. Then he looked around and found a can with a top on it and some rags. Underneath the rags there was some money, and he took it and started putting it in his shirt. I was breathing with my mouth open because every time I closed it I couldn't hardly catch my breath.

Lonnie had all the money and I thought we was going to go right then, but he was looking around in some more places. I looked up at the clock on the wall, and it said either ten minutes past ten o'clock or ten minutes past eleven o'clock. I couldn't tell which because the little hand was bent up.

"Who in there!"

I jumped when I heard that voice, and I looked over where Lonnie was. He had his finger on his lips, telling me to keep quiet. I got the hiccups but I held them in by putting my hand over my mouth and holding my breath. Then the light come on.

"Who in here!"

It was a man's voice and it sounded like he was in the room. I looked over to where Lonnie was again and he was making a sign like he wanted me to stand up. Well, I didn't want to stand up and get caught, but Lonnie kept on making that sign.

"If you don't come on out I'm gonna shoot your ass off!"

Lonnie was making a fist at me and had a terrible face on and was signing to me that I should stand up. I was crying already, and my hand was trembling and I could hardly get up, but I did.

When I stood up I saw a man, he was tall and heavy like, and he had a rifle in his hands, and I put my hands up.

"You little black bastard!" He put the rifle down and grabbed me by my hair and started punching me in the face. When he hit me I could feel some of the hair come out and taste blood in my mouth. He pushed me against the wall and hit me one more time and then he fell down. Lonnie had hit him from the back and he fell over. Lonnie pushed me towards the back room, and I started out the door and banged my knee on something. Lonnie pushed me again and I fell down, but I got right back up and we ran out the same door we had come in, up the stairs and into the hall. He grabbed me just before we got out into the street and then he stepped out and looked around.

"Yeah, so if I can get tickets we can go on down to the Garden and see the Pearl do his thing." He had his arm around my shoulder and we was walking along. He was trying to act like we didn't do nothing, but I could hardly walk because of my leg and because I was so scared. We walked over to where the park was, and then we walked along the park until we got to our block and went home.

It all happened so fast that I couldn't even think. I couldn't even think of nothing. My hands was shaking and even my shoulders was shaking a little. I felt like I was going to fall down any minute, and Lonnie kind of helped me to keep me from falling. He asked me what was the matter with me and I said my knee was hurting. But I was just weak all over. We got back to the house, and Lonnie, he pushed something down in my shirt pocket and told me to go on upstairs and get some sleep. He told me to stay there until he got back.

"You did all right," he said. "I got to give it to you, you did all right."

I went on up the stairs. I was so weak it was terrible. When I got in the house I went to the bathroom. I really had to go bad. When I finished using the bathroom, I put the television on and the radio. I don't know why I put them both on but I did.

Lonnie had some whiskey and I made a drink with the whiskey and some soda and drank that and then made another one. I started thinking about what I had done and I felt sick. I started praying to God, saying that I was sorry and things like that, and how I hope the man was all right that Lonnie hit. But then I noticed that I had the drink in my hand while I was praying, and so I quit, right in the middle of the praying, because it wasn't no use. It just wasn't no use.

I looked to see what it was that Lonnie had put in my pocket, and it was some money that we had took from the candy store. That money made me mad just being there. So I took it out and looked at it and counted it. It was twenty-one dollars. Four five-dollar bills and a one-dollar bill. I took it and balled it all up and threw it on the floor, and then I picked it up and threw it in the toilet. I started to flush the toilet when I thought I heard someone coming and thought about Lonnie. The money was going around in a circle in the toilet bowl and I grabbed at it and I got most of it but some of it got away. I reached down in the bowl but the money was gone. I felt weak again and tired. I got the money that I had grabbed and took it into the kitchen. One of the five-dollar bills and the one-dollar bill had got away. I didn't know if Lonnie wanted me to give him the money back or not. I found a book and put the money between the pages. I thought about ironing them out but I was too tired to do it. Anyway, the iron didn't work too good. I poured some more of the whiskey out and drank it and then I went to bed.

I had a dream that I was working with Lonnie and I was the one that spilled the stuff on the man and I got fired. It wasn't much of a dream.

The next day I told Lonnie I was going to go see Grandma Carrie and he asked me what for and I told him I just was. He told me that if I knew what was good for me I better keep my mouth shut. I said okay.

Before I went to see Grandma Carrie I went over to where me and Lonnie had taken the money from the candy store. It looked different in the daytime—there was a lot of kids hanging around, and some grown-ups, too. I saw a guy who used to go to the same school that I did, and I sat down on a stoop with him just down the block and across the street from where the candy store was. We just talked around a little because I didn't want to ask him about the candy store directly. He didn't say nothing about it, and then I started talking about nothing happening around the block where I lived except a man got held up two nights ago. That wasn't true, but I figured if he had heard anything about what happened in the candy store he would talk about it.

"Somebody always messing around over here," he said. "Last night some guys held up the candy store and hit Mr. Walker in his head."

"He get hurt bad?"

"Mr. Walker? No, man, you ever see that sucker's head? You got to drop a bomb on his head to hurt him," Pookie said. "They just knocked him down and dazed him for a while."

"They catch the two guys?" I asked, sorry that I had let the "two" slip out.

"Two guys?" Pookie stood up and leaned against the front of the stoop. "There was three guys, all Puerto Ricans. Mr. Walker said when he fell one of them said, 'Kill him,' so he held real still as if he was knocked out and then they left."

I sat around for a while longer, and then I told Pookie I had to split. I started up to the hospital to see Grandma Carrie and on the way I thought about what Pookie had said. I didn't know how Mr. Walker had seen three guys when there was just me and Lonnie there, and I don't look a lot like I'm Puerto Rican.

I felt a little better and a little worse as I was going to the hospital. I felt better because I didn't want them to catch me. But I felt worser, too, because now it seemed I kept thinking about things like not getting caught and worrying about police looking at me. I saw two policemen sitting in a car on Eighth Avenue, and I crossed the street and walked real slow down the other side of the street. I tried to walk natural but I didn't feel natural, I felt as if they was watching me as I went down the street. I didn't want to look around, but I did and they was gone.

That was when I decided, right then and there, that I wasn't going to go along with Lonnie any more. I thought about how we could have killed Mr. Walker even if he did have a big head. I didn't know what I was going to do if Lonnie said to come along, though. For a while I thought about having a fight with him, and then I thought about him beating me up and I knew it wasn't going to be easy. Then it come to me, all of a sudden, that I was being two people. I was being me on the outside doing things like sneaking around in Mr. Walker's place and drinking and stuff like that, and then I was being me inside looking at me on the outside doing what I was doing.

Sometimes the me on the inside was better off.

That was when I was in the house alone or just taking a walk. And sometimes the me on the outside was better off, like when I ran in the relays. But it was real hard to get the inside me and the outside me going at the same time and doing the same thing. That was mostly because the me on the inside was a whole me and that was pretty definite, but the me on the outside was what carried the inside me around. There wasn't nothing I could see to do about the outside me. I couldn't run away because I didn't have a place to run to. I couldn't change Lonnie, either, or get him a job back. When I thought that I wouldn't go around with Lonnie stealing and whatnot, I was thinking that the inside me was the real me and that I would listen to the real me. Then I thought something else. It wasn't about me, it was about Frank.

I thought that maybe there was two of him, too. Only he gave them different names, like Frank for the inside him and Motown for the outside him. And maybe he wanted to be mostly the inside him but he couldn't do it too easy either. That could be why he stayed in that place by himself. Because even if he was scared at least he was Frank and not Motown.

I asked the lady at the desk if she could send Grandma Carrie down. She was playing some cards with one of the drivers or ambulance people, and she just looked at me, started to make a phone call, and then gave me a visitor's pass.

"Room 403," she said.

I had been in the hospital before when Grandma Carrie first came in but she had been in a different room then. I took the elevator up to the fourth floor and looked around until I found 403 and went on in. She was sitting up near the window. She looked good, not sick or anything, and it made me feel kind of bad because I got a feeling like old times, when we was living together and there wasn't any problems like now.

"Hi, Grandma Carrie."

"God answers prayers." Grandma Carrie turned and looked at me, and she got tears in her eyes right away. "God answers prayers. I turned to God last night and asked Him to send you to me so I could see your face again. God answers prayers. Thank You, Jesus! Thank You, Jesus!"

"How you doing?"

"I'm doing okay, just fine." Grandma Carrie was rocking in the chair like she did when something was bothering her, and I figured that she didn't feel good and just didn't want to say it. A lot of times she didn't feel good but didn't say a lot about it.

"They gave me a pass and said I could come up," I said. "I think the nurse just didn't want to call you to come down."

"How you doing, boy?"

"Okay."

"Okay?" She just kept rocking and her mouth was tight near the corners. "You ain't doing okay, Tippy. If you was doing okay you would have come by to see your grandma. That ain't like you not to come and see your grandma."

"I'm sorry, Grandma Carrie. . . ."

"Is that boy Lonnie treating you right? You know, you the only thing I got left to love in this world. I got you and I got my Jesus." She was rocking and crying, and when I looked at her she looked old, and I hadn't noticed before but she was gray again instead of brown. I put my hand on her hand, and she looked at me and smiled a little. "You know I ain't got room in my heart to love nobody but you and your mama. I'll always love that nappy-haired girl. Long as I got a mind to remember and a little breath in me I'm gonna love her. You just like her, you know. You got her eyes in you like you took them right out that child's head. Hold your head back a little and give me a pretty smile."

She put her hand on my chin and pushed me

back a little, and I tried to smile the best I could. I tried to get my face to smiling even though I wasn't smiling inside.

"Yeah, look at you. You your mama all right. I used to call her over and say, 'Give your mama a big smile now,' and she would just smile and hug me. That girl had so much love in her that God just couldn't stand to leave her on this here earth. And you her spitting image."

She pulled me over to her like she done a lot of times before and held on to me. She used to squeeze me so I couldn't hardly breathe when she was well, but now she couldn't squeeze much, just hold on.

I felt shamed about what I was doing, about the candy store and about the drinking and everything. When she stopped holding me and we talked I told her about different things I was doing, like the races and about having the trophies. I told her I was reading a lot, too, which was not strictly true but I was reading some.

"Is God still in your heart?" she asked me.

"Yes, ma'am."

"Look me in the face, Tippy," she said. "Tell me that God is still in your heart."

"He's still in my heart, Grandma."

I wanted to tell her about the candy store, but

I knew I couldn't even fix my mouth to say those words. So I just talked about this and that and about the weather. A nurse aide came up and looked at my visitor's pass, and I told Grandma Carrie that I had to go before they found out I wasn't old enough. She said okay, but she said it in a sad way.

When I left the hospital I felt terrible. It was cloudy out and I hoped that it would rain on me or something. I even thought about getting hit by lightning. I couldn't think of nothing straight out, just stupid things, like putting my left foot in every box along the sidewalk. That's what I thought about for three whole blocks, putting my left foot in front of every box on the sidewalk as I came to it. I don't know why I thought about that. I thought about praying again—I always thought about praying when I left Grandma Carrie, I guess—but I didn't pray. There was two reasons I didn't want to. One, the sort of good reason, was that I didn't want to pray for myself, because God must have been tired of me doing what I was doing and always running around praying. The other reason was that when I thought about praying for Grandma Carrie it was a lie. Because the only thing that I could pray for her was that she got better and come home out of the hospital. But even if she did come out we probably couldn't live together again, because I heard Lonnie saying to Stone that if my grandmother got out of the hospital I was still going to live with him because that was the only way that I could be on welfare, that if I lived with her they wouldn't send a check for me because he was my father.

Another thing that was terrible but kept coming back in my head was that I didn't want Grandma Carrie to know what I was doing, or to know about it if I got caught stealing or something. And I knew that she would find out, sooner or later, if she got all right and got out of the hospital. I tried not to think about her dying, but I wanted so bad for her not to hate me and to think about me like I was that I kept thinking maybe it was better if she didn't get all right.

I had some money and thought about going to a movie but went home instead, and nobody was there so I watched some television. I laid down on the bed while I watched it and figured I would fall asleep but I didn't. I didn't want to take a drink but I did, mixing up some of the stuff that Lonnie had around the house. It wasn't good but then I found some Kool-Aid and put that in it and it wasn't bad. I had a few drinks and I felt a little better even though I was getting sick to my stomach. I remembered a picture we had seen in school about the bad things that drinking could do to you, like mess up your kidneys and some other parts. I remembered they showed pictures of people laying in the streets, and I thought about myself laying in the streets and people coming over to me and picking me up. Then I must have fallen to sleep because the next thing I know Lonnie was waking me up.

"Hey, man, get up!" he said.

I opened my eyes and the room was spinning around and I felt like I was gonna throw up.

"What you been doing?" Lonnie yelled at me right in my ear. He had been drinking, and I hoped he wasn't going to start pushing me around, but he was.

He slapped me in the face, and at first I started to go right past him to go to the bathroom, and he kept slapping me even when I went out into the other room. Denise was in the other room and Stone and Bubba. He kept on hitting me and saying things like what was I, a drunk or something. I started to fight him back and then he punched me in the stomach. When he did that I started throwing up and he kept hitting me. I slid along the wall until I got to the bathroom.

Denise was screaming and carrying on and was trying to get him to stop hitting me. I got into the bathroom and she came in with me and sat on the edge of the tub while I was throwing up. Then she helped me to wash up. I looked at her and she was crying worser than I was. I got myself fixed up and when I came out of the bathroom Lonnie was sitting at the table looking mad. I still didn't know what I had done to make him mad. I didn't tell nobody about the candy store or nothing.

He told me to clean up the mess I made. I looked at him and then I ran on out the door and down the stairs. He started out after me, but he stumbled on one of the steps and couldn't catch up with me.

I ran out into the street and then I walked over to Mr. Roland's house but nobody was home. I looked in my pocket and saw that I still had some of the money I had from before, and so I got on the subway and went down to 42nd Street to the movies. I saw the same picture I had seen before about space ships and whatnot. It was a good picture to see because it took your mind off whatever you were thinking about, even if you saw it before. I was going to see it two times, too, but then it got boring the second time and I left.

I was very tired, about as tired as I had ever been. I went over to the park near the library but people kept bothering me so I left because I didn't want to be bothered. Then I just walked around for a while until I got over to 43rd Street, where the newspaper offices was. Across the street from the newspaper offices there was a old building where nobody lived, and I thought that maybe I could go into it and stay like Frank stayed in that other building in Brooklyn. I waited around until nobody was looking, and then I went into it through a door that was open. I could hear some noises in it, like maybe mice or rats was running around, and I couldn't see nothing. It was pitch-black in there, and so I went out again and went over and bought a flashlight and a candy bar and went back.

I turned out the flashlight after I found a room and a chair to sit in. I had to keep turning it on again when I kept hearing all kinds of noises around the place, though.

I thought to myself about what I was going to do with myself, and I thought about running away and going out to California or maybe Ohio or someplace like that. But then I was thinking that it wouldn't be no different than going to 42nd Street, like I was doing now.

I thought about other things, too, like beating up Lonnie and then running away. I wondered if he would shoot me if I did beat him up. I didn't think so. I thought I could run away with Denise, but I didn't know if Bubba would be mad or if she would even run away with me, but I thought that she liked me. I knew she liked me a little, anyway.

At first I could hear the noises from the streets, like car noises or truck noises, things like that. After a while I could still hear them but not as many. The cars was hissing, like it was raining outside, but I couldn't hear people talking. I still heard noises, and then I heard something like somebody creeping around the building. I told myself that it was just my imagination, but I still thought I could hear it. Every time I stopped thinking to listen real careful it would stop moving. I knew I was going to be scared, but I was even scareder than I thought I was going to be. I decided that maybe I would leave the building. I thought about Frank, how he always stayed in that building by himself, and wondered if he was ever scared.

It took me a long time to get down the stairs because I kept looking around in case something jumped out at me from the shadows. I was glad that I had bought the flashlight because I would have been too scared to even move without it.

When I got to the door where I had come in, I jumped right out of it. There was some guys sitting against the building, and they all jumped when I jumped over them. One had a bottle and I could hear it break as I ran on down the street. I must have scared them pretty bad.

It wasn't nearly as late as I thought it was but it was already getting dark. I tried to figure out something to do with myself but I couldn't. I thought that must be the hardest thing to do if you run away or be alone a lot—figuring out what to do with yourself.

It was raining a little, not much, but I thought it might rain a lot more. I had to go to the bathroom, too. I always did when it started to rain. I went into the bus station and looked around to see if they had a bathroom. They did and I went in. There was some men just standing around in there, and I felt kind of nervous with the way they was looking. When I came out I saw people sitting around and waiting for buses. I sat around like I was waiting for a bus, trying to think what I should do.

"Would you be interested in reading about the life of the Lord Krishna?"

I jumped a little because I didn't see this guy come and sit down next to me. He was dressed in a robe or something. It was yellow and most of his hair was cut off except for a little patch right on top his head.

I said no, mainly because I didn't know what he was talking about.

"If I offered you truth, would you refuse it?" he asked. He was smiling, and I thought maybe he was making a joke because I didn't see why he was smiling.

"No," I said.

"Well, that's what I'm offering you," he said, "the truth."

Then he showed me this magazine with paintings in it. He started explaining to me what the paintings was about. I saw another one, just like this guy, talking to some other people, which made me feel better. He kept on talking and showing me the magazine. All the time he was looking at me I would look at the magazine, but when he looked down at the magazine I looked at his head. He was white and where his hair was supposed to be it was all gray. He had some white marks on his forehead, too. I tried to listen to him for a while and understand what he was saying, but then another guy come up.

"The brother doesn't need you, Satan!"

This was the other guy, only he was black and he had on a white robe like a Arab. It even went over his head and everything. He had a magazine, too. He also had some incense and a can with a slot on top where you could put some money in it.

"He does not need me," the guy with the yellow

robe said, "but he does need Lord Krishna."

"Allah will be his salvation." The black guy with the white robe put his hand on my shoulder.

"The Lord God is called by many names," the guy in the yellow robe said. Then he put his hand on my other shoulder.

"The minds of our young black brothers shall not be in your hands, Satan," white robe said. "The Koran tells us to beware the infidel."

"Lord Krishna tells us not to abandon the soul of man, even to his own wickedness." The guy in the yellow robe was still smiling.

"Take your hands off the brother, chump!" the guy in the white robe said, and he pushed the other guy's hand away. The other guy pushed the white robe's hand off my other shoulder, and then they started fighting.

The guy in the white robe was bigger, but the guy in the yellow robe got him down and was on top of him until the guy in the white robe stuck one of his incense things in the other guy's eye. Then they was rolling around on the floor. It was funny seeing them roll around like that, with their robes on and everything, but I figured I would leave anyway.

I went down a little way and turned around, and there was a little crowd of people standing around watching them fight. No one was too excited-looking. Then another lady came up to me—she was wearing a sign and asked me if I knew that I might not even have been born if everybody believed in free abortions. Then she said that Jesus loved everybody and wanted everybody to be born. She asked me would I sign a paper.

I wasn't too sure what she was talking about, either. But I wanted to sign the paper because of what she said about Jesus and everything. But then I didn't have a chance to because she saw some other people walking by and she had to hurry over and get them. I hung around the bus station for a while longer and then I left. I got to the train platform just as my train got there.

I figured that Lonnie might give me a hard time again, but I didn't know what else to do or where to go to. I thought for a little while about going over to Mr. Roland's house but then I would have to tell him a long story so I didn't. I thought about going to Denise's house, and that seemed like a good idea. She could tell me if Lonnie was still mad, too.

When I got up to her house it was almost a quarter to ten. She wasn't sitting on the stoop, like she usually did, and I thought she might not be home. Two other ladies was sitting on the stoop. Sometimes Denise didn't like to be around other people because she said they kept trying to get into her business. I went up to Denise's house and knocked and after a while she answered the door. She had on a bathrobe, and her eyes was wide. I said hello, and she stood in the doorway, and I asked if I could come in, and she said not right then. Then I saw somebody move in the back and it was Stone.

I asked Denise if Lonnie was still home, and she said yes. Then she told me that she and Bubba had had a fight. I said oh, and then I was going to leave, but when I was about halfway down the steps from her floor Stone came out and called to me.

"Hey, little brother." He was acting friendly. I didn't like Stone before, and now that he was fooling around with Denise I really didn't like him.

"What you want?"

"Where you going?"

"Home."

"Hey, what's the deal?" He sat down on the steps and put his arm around me. I could smell he was smoking herb. "Hey, look, man, Denise and Bubba was having a fight, and I came up and tried to get it straight, see? But I don't want Bubba to know because I don't want him to think I'm getting into his business, see?"

"Yeah, I see."

He reached into his pocket and pulled out a five-dollar bill and a one-dollar bill and put the one-dollar bill into my shirt pocket, then he went back up to Denise's house. I watched him go on in and Denise looked down at me for a while before she closed the door. I wasn't in love with her or anything like that, but I liked her a lot. I used to, anyway.

I threw the dollar away on the way home. I just threw it in the street. I didn't want anything from Stone.

When I got home Bubba was there with Lonnie and they was smoking herb, too. I started to go into my room and Lonnie got up and started toward the room, too. I figured he was going to beat on me again, but I knew I was tired and figured if I just took it for a while then I would fall asleep soon after. He couldn't hit so hard when he was high, anyway.

"Look, man." Lonnie sat on the bed. He just had his shorts on, and the top part of his leg spread out over three and a half squares when he sat down. When I sat down my leg could hardly cover up one and a half squares. "I'm sorry I hit you."

I didn't say nothing, and he just sat there for a while, and I tried to think about something else.

"Hey, man, look." He put his hand on my leg like that was supposed to mean something. "I just don't want to see you drinking and everything, see. Because it ain't right. I mean, I drink and I smoke herb, and that ain't right, either, but I already done blew my thing, dig?

"You still got some more to go. You can't . . . you can't . . . you know, blow your thing when you only your age, see. Now me, it don't make much difference if I blow my thing or not because it just don't matter. I don't like to see you mess your life up, see, because, you can still do things, and what-not. Maybe you can get a scholarship and that kind of thing. A running scholarship or even one of the scholarships they gives out for taking tests. You got all that, man?

"And I ain't gonna say that I'm gonna be a good example, see, but I know what's right and what's not right. That's definite. That's on the money."

He kept on talking and talking like he was afraid to stop because I would think he wasn't telling the truth or something. He couldn't but half get it out anyway. Even if he hadn't been smoking the herb he couldn't talk much better. I thought about how he had messed up and lost his job by spilling the stuff on the salesman, and how he must have tried to talk straight then and couldn't.

I could understand what he was trying to say, that he didn't want me to mess up the way he did, and I thought that he meant it, too, but it didn't make a lot of difference. It didn't make a lot of difference because he still didn't have a job and he was still Lonnie and had his ways, and I was still me.

Grandma Carrie used to always say that you could better yourself if you really wanted to, but I couldn't even think of nothing for Lonnie to do. He was doing okay with his friends, like Bubba and Stone and them, but he wasn't doing okay with people who wasn't his friends. Maybe that was the trouble—they wasn't his friends.

Then he started talking about just one more big job and everything would be cool. I didn't know nothing else for him to do, and I felt sorry for him and everything, but stealing just made me feel like I wasn't nothing at all. Because every time I used to look at somebody who stole things or did other bad things I could say at least I didn't do that. Even if they was better-looking or had better clothes. Now I couldn't say anything. I never liked people who stole things, not even because of God and the Bible saying it was wrong—I just didn't think it was the right way to live. I didn't like people who lived like that, and now I didn't like me very much either. I wasn't very mad at Lonnie, though. I don't know why. I could tell he wanted me to say it was okay for him to pull one more job, and I wanted to, because he wanted me to pretty bad, but I couldn't do it. I thought I was being not forgiving, or like casting a first stone or something, but I didn't say nothing to make it easier.

Later, when Bubba left, Lonnie asked me if I wanted to watch some television. I didn't say nothing but I sat down in Lonnie's room and watched it some. In a little while he fell asleep and I went in to bed.

14

"**Well, we got** it all planned out," Lonnie said. I had just made some tea and was looking for someplace to put the bag so it wouldn't stain the table.

"You got what all planned out?"

"What we gonna do to get us some money," he said. "You part of the plan."

I dumped the tea in the sink. "I ain't no thief."

"What you mean, you ain't no thief!" Lonnie looked at me and put on his scary voice, but it didn't scare me as much as it did sometimes. "You calling me a thief?"

"You steal," I said, trying to look at him out of the side of my eyes. I didn't want to look at him right in the face, but I wanted to look at him in case he tried to hit me.

"In other words, what you trying to say"—he came over kind of close to me and sat down so that his leg was touching mine—"is that because I want to pull one last job so I can get some money and make something out of myself you gonna put me down. That's right, huh?"

I didn't say nothing back but I felt a little good about him sitting so close to me. I figured that when he sat close to me like that he knew I was going to be afraid and that's why he did it. If he had to make me afraid of him, then I knew I was right.

"I thought you wanted me to go straight so we could live better," he said. "You like living in this place?"

"It's okay with me," I said. It wasn't great but it wasn't terrible.

"Sheeee. . . . Ain't you got nothin' in you smell like a damn man?"

He was really trying to get me scared and he was doing it. I just knew he was going to hit me again, but he didn't. He just leaned over real close to me and asked me if I was going to do what they told me.

I said yes. I was just tired of getting beat up all the time, so I told him I would do it. He said maybe I would be a man after all. I said, "The hell with you," only I said it in my mind because I didn't want him to knock my teeth out.

I got really mad when we was sitting around waiting for Stone and them to come to the house. I was mad at myself, mostly, but really more mad than I had ever been.

They was going to do it on a Thursday night. It was going to be Lonnie, Bubba, Stone, me, and a white girl named Jackie. Stone copied out a big map on a piece of paper and he said what everybody was supposed to do. It was like on television, with everybody sitting around the table nodding their heads and stuff.

"Okay, let's go over this mother one more time," Stone said. "This time everybody tell me they part. Start with you, Lonnie."

"I got the guard uniform on. When you give me the signal me and Jackie walk up to the night-deposit thing and get there just before he do. Then I get the drop on the dude he be with."

"Right." Stone gave Lonnie five. "Go on, Jackie."

"Okay. Me and Lonnie walk up and I say to the guy, 'You mind if I make a deposit first?' Then I step up in front of the night-deposit box and make like I'm looking for my key."

"Right. Go on, Bubba."

"I'm walking up the other way like I'm just walking past, and when I see Lonnie get the drop on the sucker I get the drop on the cat with the bread and take it."

"Right. Go on, Tippy."

"I look down the block and see when they come out of the store and then I take my hat off."

"Right," Stone said. "When Tippy see them coming out the store he takes his hat off. I see him and give you the sign. You wait five or ten seconds and then you go on up to the deposit box. When he sees you in the guard uniform he'll hurry on up there 'cause he figures it's safe, especially you with a white girl. This young dude always goes with him but I don't know if he carries a piece or not. You get the drop on the guy just in case."

"Don't you think we should be wearing masks or something?" Lonnie asked.

"What for?" Stone asked. "All the cat gonna say is that a tall, dark-skin Negro did it. That fits half the people in the damn city. Don't be jiving with no masks. Soon as you and Bubba get near this dude I'm gonna start the car up and get over to you. You snatch the sucker's bag with the money and then shoot at the cat's feet or something and everybody get in the car. We go a block and pick up Tippy on the corner and then we split to where I got the other car parked.

"Jackie, you get out and take the money and the guns to my house in the other car—Bubba, you go with her. Me, Lonnie, and Tippy'll go over to Lonnie's place. Jackie, you let Bubba out at the first subway stop. That way you'll just be another white girl in the car and we'll all be separated. We all meet back here at one o'clock. Everybody got that straight?"

"Yeah," Bubba said, and everybody else nodded.

"How much money you say this guy got?" Lonnie asked.

"He works in that liquor store right off Queens Boulevard so he got to have a nice little taste. We'll be pulling this job tonight, and today is welfare-check day so the sucker'll be loaded. It's going to be a nice taste. Okay, Lonnie, you and Jackie go on. Keep the guard jacket and the hat and stick in the bag until you get near the place. Don't come up until I give you the signal.

"Bubba, you and Tippy go on out and you show him what corner to stand on and where the liquor store is so he can see the cat come out and close it up. Let's go."

It was exciting and I was nervous. I saw Denise when I went downstairs with Bubba. Bubba gave her a big kiss and said that he would see her later. She said she was going to give me a kiss, since she gave Bubba one, but I pulled away because I was still mad at her for fooling around with Stone.

We got the D train downtown to 42nd Street

and then we got the F train out to a place called 75th Avenue. It was nice. The streets was clean and there wasn't too many people in the streets. The ones that was was mostly older white people and only one or two black people. We walked around for a while because it wasn't even near the right time yet, and Bubba told me that he had a job out here once painting the seats where they play tennis. He said he could play tennis, too, but I didn't believe him. We just walked around for a while looking at the stores and everything, and I asked him how come Lonnie was wearing the uniform. Bubba said it was because Stone had to drive and he had a tooth missing in the front of his mouth and most guards got all their teeth. He also said that his tooth got knocked out when he was trying out for the Olympic boxing team, and I didn't believe that, either. The only person he could beat up with his skinny self was Denise.

It got to be about the time and Bubba took me to a corner and pointed out the liquor store. It was still open and I could see people going in and out of it. He said it would be about fifteen minutes more before it closed. He still stood around with me for a while, and I asked him if he was in love with Denise.

"I can't love nobody," he said. "A girl broke

my heart once and I ain't never loved again."

"Oh."

After a while he walked away and I was standing at the corner all by myself. The people looked kind of nice walking by, except for now there wasn't very many people at all. One lady went by with two little dogs with ribbons on, and they looked frisky and cute. She let them stop near me for a minute because she saw me looking at them and then she went on by.

I looked around to see if I could see anybody else, and the only person I could see was Bubba. I couldn't even see Stone, and I wondered if they had got there. I was leaning against the post, on one leg, and I started daydreaming about going to Australia, because I had seen a picture about Australia on television. I must have been daydreaming for a while because when I got back to where I was the liquor store was dark. I looked down the street and I didn't see nobody and I thought I had really messed up. I didn't know if I should take the hat off or not. I looked down the street and I saw that Bubba was still where he was before and I didn't see nobody else.

I looked back to the liquor store and it was still dark, and I looked up the street the other way and I still couldn't see nobody. I started walking across the street to tell Bubba, when the liquor store opened and two men came out. Then I took my hat off and went back across the street. One of the men stooped down real quick and did something at the bottom of the door and then they started walking toward me, only on the other side of the street. They turned the corner and walked down the block to where Bubba had been, but he was gone. The two men was talking to each other as they walked down the street and not paying any attention to nobody. Then I saw Lonnie and Jackie come walking up and Lonnie had on the guard uniform and Bubba was walking across the street. It was like a movie. When they all got together I couldn't hear nothing, but I saw the men give a little jump and Bubba pushed one of the men. Then the car came up and I heard some shooting. They all got into the car and the car came down near where I was and stopped and I started getting in and Lonnie grabbed me and pulled me in real quick. Just when he did that the glass in the back broke. I was laying across everybody and Jackie was screaming in the front seat.

"Get the door! Get the door!" she kept shouting out. I got off somebody's legs and half turned around, and Jackie who was sitting in the front seat and Lonnie who was sitting in the back was both reaching for the back door which was still open. Stone turned the car down a street and the door came close to them and they grabbed it and slammed it shut.

I looked up at Lonnie and he was sweating, trying to look out the back window. Sweat was running down the side of his face. Bubba was leaning against the window. You could hear him breathing real hard and his forehead was wrinkled up like he was hurting.

"Oh, my God!" Jackie twisted around in the seat and put her hand on Bubba.

"Where you hit, man?" Lonnie asked.

"In the side." Bubba answered him back with his eyes closed.

The car went around the corner, making us all go to one side, and me and Lonnie got thrown onto Bubba and he screamed out. Jackie screamed out again, too. Finally Stone slowed the car down and we got off of Bubba.

"Jackie, you get out at the subway," Stone said. "You go with her, Lonnie. Then I'll take Bubba over to your house."

"I can help with Bubba." Jackie was taking a handkerchief and wiping some white stuff from Bubba's mouth.

"Don't want you in the car," Stone said. "They gonna be stopping every car they see with a nigger and a white chick in it. You go on home and I'll call you later when everything gets cool."

"How about me?" I asked.

"Let him stay with me, Lonnie."

Lonnie said okay. We pulled over to a subway entrance and Jackie and Lonnie got out. I got up in the front seat with Stone. Bubba laid across the back seat. He was still breathing hard and he was holding his stomach. Stone kept telling him to "hang on, man" and things like that.

"The pain'll ease up after a while. We get to Lonnie's house we can get some stuff for you. I got some painkiller I got from the dentist. You smoke a couple of J's and that'll put you to sleep. We'll stay with you and see how you doing. If things don't look copacetic we'll get you a doctor. You feeling any better?"

"No, man, this pain is something else."

"Yeah, it be's that way," Stone said. "Sometimes it really be's that way. We scooped enough cash to lay up for a while, maybe you can take Denise down to Puerto Rico. You ever been to Puerto Rico?"

"Naw."

"Puerto Rico's boss, real boss. Lay out on the

beach soaking up all that sun. Be back on your feet before you know it."

"We far from Lonnie's?"

"Yeah," I answered. Stone gave me a look.

"We ain't that far. We got to wait until they get there. We can't be sitting on the stoop waiting for the sucker."

Stone drove around for a while longer, and then he was in Manhattan and driving towards the house. It was late and there wasn't too many people on the street when we pulled up to the house.

"Hey, Bubba, wake up, man."

"I'm awake."

"Look, we at Lonnie's house. You got to act like you okay until we get inside the house, dig?"

"I can't make it."

"Then I got to leave you outside in the car."

"C'mon, Stone, that ain't right." Bubba pushed himself up and took a deep breath. His face twisted when he breathed in and I saw there was more white stuff dried up around his mouth.

"I'll help you in," Stone said. "You ready?"

Bubba nodded. I wondered where Lonnie was. Stone got out of the car and came around and opened the door to Bubba's side.

"C'mon, man." Stone spoke in a loud voice.

"This is the second time in a row you done got drunk in my car. Why don't you go on and sleep it off?"

Bubba got out the car kind of bent over and Stone put his arm around him and helped him up the steps. When we got in the vestibule we heard steps and Stone put his hand in his pocket, like he had a gun in there or something, but it was Lonnie. Lonnie and Stone helped Bubba up the stairs and they put him on my bed. Then Stone told Lonnie that he had to go get rid of the car and Lonnie said okay.

Lonnie put some blankets on Bubba and put the television on so he could see it. They put on the news and Lonnie told me to watch it and call him if I heard anything. Then he went to the bathroom. I sat in the room with Bubba, mostly listening to the way he was breathing. He breathed very regular and I almost forgot I was listening to it except for one time I didn't hear him breathe and it scared me, but he started up again.

They didn't have anything on the television about what we had done. After a while Stone came back and he put the radio on and gave Bubba the pills he had got from his dentist. Then Jackie came by and gave Bubba some herb to smoke. Bubba smoked the herb and then he said he felt better. Stone, who had kind of taken over, said to let him get some rest and we all left my room.

"What went down, anyway?" Stone asked.

"Lonnie got the drop on the young dude and when he started to put his hands up we saw a piece in his belt, and Lonnie took it," Jackie said. "Then we took the deposit bag from the old dude and we started towards the car. Bubba shoots down at the ground like you said, and then all of a sudden all hell broke loose!"

"The old guy pulled a piece and just started shooting away. I shot back and then I jumped into the car," Lonnie said.

"Did you kill him?" I asked, holding my breath and hoping that he would say no.

"No, man," Lonnie said. I looked at his face to see if he looked like he was telling the truth.

"Hey, baby, that's definitely not the deal," Jackie said. She put her hand on mine but it didn't mean nothing to me at all.

Then they counted up all the money they had, and it was close to two thousand dollars, and each one was going to get five hundred dollars. Jackie said she thought there should be more than that and Stone said there was, but some of it was in checks and he didn't want to mess with them.

Stone told Lonnie not to say nothing about Bubba's being up to our house to Denise. Then he and Jackie left. I had to sleep with Lonnie—it was the first time that I had ever slept with anybody except Grandma Carrie. I couldn't sleep anyway. I kept expecting the police to come and start banging on the door. I wasn't too worried about Bubba because Stone had looked at the place he was shot and said that it didn't look too bad. Stone had been shot before and he was okay, too.

The next morning I got up as soon as it was light out and made some tea for Lonnie and me and some eggs. I woke him up when they was ready. He asked me how I slept and I said not too good. He said he didn't sleep too good either. I went out and got the paper and we looked through it and didn't see nothing about what had happened. But when we listened to the radio it told about it.

It said that three men and a girl held up a guy by the name of Sal Cushman and had got away with over five thousand dollars. I looked at Lonnie and felt terrible. They didn't mention my name or anything or even mention that I was there, but they knew Lonnie was there, or at least they knew about what he had did, and was talking about it all over the radio. I wondered if Grandma Carrie was listening to the radio in the hospital.

I asked Lonnie how come they said that there was five thousand dollars stolen when there was only two thousand and he said he didn't know. I had forgot about Bubba and I went in to see him, to see how he was doing, and he wasn't doing good at all. He was real ashy and weak-looking. He said he had to go to the bathroom and he could get up by himself, but when he was in the bathroom he called me and Lonnie and we went in to see what was the matter. He pointed to the toilet and there was some blood in the water.

"That ain't nothing to worry about," Lonnie said. "That's just a strain."

I didn't know if it was just a strain or not but Bubba kept getting worse. He said he was in a lot of pain. Lonnie told him to try to get as much sleep as he could. Later on Lonnie told me to sit with Bubba while he went and looked for Stone. I put on the stories for him and we watched them together and he told me about the different people in them. Bubba knew everyone in all the stories.

"That chick is messing around with that other

chick's husband and she don't even know it," he said. "When she find out she's going to cut him off without a cent. She's got all the money, you know."

He talked about them just like they was real, everyday, walking-around people. It was the only thing that seemed to cheer him up a little.

Stone came back up and he and Lonnie talked to Bubba and Bubba said he felt bad. Stone told him that he had to hang on, but Bubba kept saying that he wanted to go to a hospital.

"You can't go to no hospital," Stone said. "Soon as they see a bullet wound they turn you over to the cops."

"You can just take me to the hospital and then I'll say I got mugged," Bubba said.

It wasn't so much what Bubba was saying but the way he said it that begin to bother me. He was saying it like he was scared. I don't like to see people scared, because when they scared it means they think something bad's going to happen to them. I knew Bubba was thinking that he might die. Stone said he was going to get a man he knew that could take out bullets but I didn't believe it. Me and Lonnie was eating some fried chicken we had bought already fried up when we heard a noise in my room, where Bubba was. We went in and Bubba had fallen over the bed. He had his pants on and was trying to leave but he had fell down instead. We helped him back up on the bed and he said he wanted to go home.

"I don't even want that money," he said. He reached under the pillow where he was keeping his share of the money and threw it near the foot of the bed where Lonnie was standing. "Honest, man."

"Stone said he would be right back," Lonnie said. "Take it easy."

Bubba leaned back against the pillow and closed his eyes. I felt sorry for him.

I didn't think that Stone was coming back but he did. He brought a guy with him and he and the guy and me and Lonnie went in to look at Bubba. The guy helped Bubba turn over and looked at the place where he got hit by the bullet. I looked, too. It was a little hole and you didn't think that it would hurt much.

"It don't look bad," Stone said. "What you think?"

The guy, who was real fat and wore thick glasses, looked at the hole real close and said it wasn't infected or nothing. Then he told Bubba to lay over on his back.

"When I do that my back hurts something

awful," Bubba said. "I can't even stand it."

"You got any more of them pills I give you?" Stone asked.

"Yeah, I still got some."

While they was talking I looked at Bubba's stomach—it was regular on one side but swoll up on the other side. The guy just touched it a little bit, with one finger, and Bubba liked to jump out of the bed.

"Oh, Lord!" he screamed. Stone ran up to the top of the bed and I thought he was going to put his hand over Bubba's mouth or something but he didn't. I think he was thinking of it, though.

"What he got, a little infection on his side?" Stone asked.

"Yeah," the man said, looking at Bubba. Then he reached down and threw the cover on Bubba.

"Hey, man, can you do anything about it?" Bubba tried to get himself up on one elbow.

"It'll be okay," the guy said. "Just get a lot of rest." Then he just walked out of the room.

"I told you everything was going to be cool," Stone said. "Didn't I tell you that?"

"Yeah, you said it," Bubba said, but his heart wasn't in it.

"I'll get some more pain pills from this guy and you can lay up and rest a taste," Stone said.

"You want the money to pay him?" Bubba asked. Lonnie had put the money back up under the pillow and Bubba took it out again and held it out to Stone.

"Hey, keep your money," Stone said. "I can get these pills from this cat for nothing. No sweat."

Then he told Bubba to get some rest and we all went into the other room where the guy was waiting.

"So what's the story?" Stone asked the guy.

"A hundred and fifty dollars," he said.

"A hundred and fifty dollars for *what?*" Lonnie had started to put water in the kettle for coffee and stopped when the guy said a hundred and fifty dollars.

"This ain't no Blue Cross visit." The guy took off his glasses and he had narrow little eyes that was close together. "That guy got a bad infection and he got to be drained. Even if you drain him he can kick off."

"Maybe we ought to take him to the hospital and leave him like he said," Lonnie said.

"You got to be jiving. All they got to do is touch him and he start squawking like a damn pig. He'd turn his mama in. We take him to the hospital we all going to the slam!"

"Where my hundred and fifty?" the piggy-looking guy said.

"What hundred and fifty?" Stone said. "You didn't do nothing!"

"I'll walk on out of here with nothing if you want me to." The guy who had looked at Bubba put his glasses back on and looked around the room. "But I ain't going to be happy about it. And if I ain't happy when I walk out of here you ain't going to be happy when I walk out of here."

"Sheee . . . !" Stone let out a low whistling noise. Then he pulled some money out, counted it, and dropped it on the floor in front of the piggy guy.

The piggy guy bent over real quick, scooped the money up, and counted it with little grunting noises.

"Twen'y . . . fo'ty . . . si'ty . . . eighty . . . ni'ty . . . huner . . . huner-twen'y . . . huner-fo'ty . . . yeah." Then he left.

"He won't say nothing," Lonnie said. "I know Bubba, he's all right."

"What you talking about?" Stone asked.

"About us leaving Bubba to the hospital."

"Now that case is closed," Stone said. "I ain't going to jail for no damn jive."

"So what we gonna do?" Lonnie asked.

"Nothing, man," Stone said. "We going to sit down, have us a J, and relax. There's nothing we can do for the cat. If there was something we could do for him I'd a done it right off. Now we got to wait and see what happens. If he pulls through that, everything's okay. If he don't we got to take him out and do something with him."

When Stone said that he sat down and crossed his legs and took his jacket off. He had a gun in his belt. He rolled a J and lit it and took a drag. Then he handed it over to Lonnie.

"I don't want it," Lonnie said. He was drinking his coffee.

"Now what does *that* mean?" Stone asked.

"I just don't want it."

Stone flicked the J at Lonnie and it hit him on the arm. Lonnie started to stand up and Stone put his hand on his gun.

"Sit down, man."

"What you got your hand on your piece for?" Lonnie said.

"What you acting so damn funny for?" Stone said. "I thought you was a down cat—now you want to mess everything up."

"I said what you got your hand on your piece for?" Lonnie said again.

"Find out, man," Stone said. "Do something I tell you not to do and find out!"

Stone and Lonnie just looked at each other for

a while. Lonnie was halfway standing up and halfway sitting down. Stone was sitting up with his hand on the gun. Then Lonnie sat down and leaned against the wall and looked at a magazine. Stone rolled another J and lit it up. Lonnie looked at the magazine and then at another one and then he picked up the J off the floor and lit it up.

"Hey, Tippy!" It was Bubba calling me. At first I didn't want to go in there with him but then I went in.

"How you doing?" I asked.

"Okay," he said. "Why don't you put the television on?"

I put the television on and a program was just going off and another program, called *The Gong Show,* was just coming on.

"Hey, man, you ever dig this *Gong Show*?"

"Yeah."

"Man, they got some funny mess on this program. One time they had this fat chick dressed up like a bird. Man, she couldn't sing wortha two cents but she came on out and sang anyway. You should have seen that chick. This cat here, not that one, that one on the left . . . he took a look at that fat chick and just cracked up laughing. Every time the camera was on him he was just laughing away, man. And see this cat?"

"Yeah."

"That cat's cold. He gonged a little old woman one time and the whole audience was booing on him and everything. You know what I mean?"

"Yeah."

"He gonged her ass anyway, though. He a cold cat. Usually when they have a brother on the show or a sister they be pretty cool—you ever notice that?"

"Yeah." The television was jiggling around and I fixed the picture by hanging a coat hanger on the antenna. Then it worked pretty good.

"This cat can't sing a lick," Bubba said. There was a tall, skinny guy singing on the television.

"That's opera, though," I said. "They might like it."

"No, that chick's getting ready to gong him now," Bubba said. "Watch her."

We watched the guy sing, and they didn't gong him, and he got twenty-five points. Then the commercial came on.

"Say, what they talking about out there?" Bubba asked.

"Just this and that," I said. "I think they getting high."

"They say I'm gonna be all right?"

"Yeah."

"I hope this thing don't take forever. I got to go down South and see my people before the summer is over, you know what I mean?"

"Yeah. I didn't know you had people down South."

"All niggers got people down South. You might not know who they is but you got people down South. What that cat say was here before?"

"What cat?"

"That guy who looked at me?"

"Him?"

"Yeah."

"Something about a infection."

"That ain't nothing, right?"

"Right."

"Lonnie think it's a infection?"

"I guess so."

"He ain't worried or nothing, is he?" Bubba said. "He ain't scared?"

"No."

"Me and Lonnie been tight a long time, man. We go way back," Bubba said. "You know that?"

"Oh, yeah?"

"Yeah."

We kept on watching *The Gong Show* and I started thinking about a girl I used to know that everybody called Nose. She wasn't good-looking at all and everybody teased because she had this big nose. Then one time her mother came to school about something and her mother had been drinking. Then they called her elephant nose and said that she and her mother used their noses for sucking up whiskey. That was bad but it wasn't so bad because everybody talked about each other some. But one day Patricia—that was her real name—didn't come to school and in the afternoon we found out that she had jumped out the window of the projects.

I felt bad about that and wondered what was so bad that made her kill herself. When I was sitting next to Bubba and looking at that television show and thinking about Lonnie and Stone in the next room, I thought that if I had to live like that all my life maybe I would jump out the window, too. Especially if Bubba died.

I didn't want Bubba to die. If he died because nobody helped him, then I would be one of the ones that didn't help him. And I would almost be the main one because I knew I was not supposed to be this way. I didn't know about how Stone and Lonnie was supposed to be.

I thought if Bubba died, then I would have to do everything that Stone and Lonnie said because I was there when he died and was part of it. Just the same way that they was a part of it I'd be a part, and it didn't matter if they was bigger than me or even if they had a gun. Because you can't go back to not knowing things, and the things you know about yourself is what makes you one way or the other.

All that thinking was good but I was still scared of Lonnie and Stone. I had a feeling like the inside me was saying I had to do something or there wouldn't be a inside me any more. I made myself think about Bubba dying. About having to take him outside, like Stone said, and leaving him in some lonely place. I wondered if dead people would feel lonely. I thought if they knew anything after they was dead, it would be about being lonely, and being left somewhere or put in the ground.

I tried thinking of something to do. I thought about running and jumping out the window. Maybe I wouldn't die and everyone would want to know what was going on and then they would come up and save Bubba. But I didn't want to jump out the window, not really. Because I didn't want to die and I thought I might.

I also thought about throwing a book or something at the window, but it might not break and even if it did nobody might come up. People were always fighting and breaking windows. Then I got a idea, but I didn't think I was going to be able to do it because I got scared just thinking about it.

"I bet this guy gonna win," Bubba said.

I looked up at the television and there was a young guy on there with a dinner suit on. He looked like he was probably going to win. "I'll see you a little later," I said to Bubba.

"Hey, man, don't leave," Bubba said. "Wait until this is over."

"I got to go now," I said. "I'll be back."

I went on into the other room where Stone and Lonnie was still sitting around smoking herb. I went over to the refrigerator and looked in. There was a bottle with a little whiskey in it. I pushed some things around in the refrigerator like I was looking for something, and then I pushed the bottle behind a large jar of mayonnaise.

"How's my man doing in there?" Stone asked.

"Okay, I guess," I said. "We got anything to drink?"

"You looking where we keep the stuff!" Lonnie said.

"Ain't nothing here but soda and milk," I said, trying to be cool.

"That's all you need, sucker!" I didn't even look up at Lonnie, because I knew how he was looking.

"I'm going over to Denise's house to get some wine," I said, closing the refrigerator door.

"Sit your ass down!" Lonnie said.

"I'll be back in a while," I said, like I didn't even hear him.

He must have jumped over the table or something because the next thing I knew I felt something hit me on the side of my face and I fell down under the sink. There was a ringing in my ears and for a moment I couldn't see just where I was. He grabbed me and pulled me up and I tried to push away from him. He just pushed my hand away and punched me again and I got real dizzy. He might have hit me again, but I'm not too sure. Anyway, I was on the floor on my knees and was getting sick to my stomach like the last time he beat up on me.

When my eyes were okay again, I saw Lonnie's shoes in front of me and I was hoping he wouldn't kick me. He picked his foot up and put it on me and pushed me over again. I rolled over on my back and looked over to where Stone was sitting and saw him looking at me, and I felt even smaller than I was.

"Get over there and sit down!" Lonnie said. This time his voice was like hoarse.

I got myself up real slow and I stood looking

at Lonnie. He was smelling like herb and cigarettes. He looked back at me, like he always did,
like he was as mad as he could be. Only this time
I wasn't scared, not even a little bit. It was like he
had pushed me right past being scared and right
past being hurt. I was already hurt—I could feel
my nose bleeding and the side of my face was
jumping from where he hit me.

"I ain't going back over to no place and sit
down," I said. "You want to hit me again you go
right on and do it, 'cause that's the only thing you
got left to do to me."

"You think I won't?" He was shouting out.
"You think I won't?"

I went and picked my hat up off the table and
walked on out the door. I thought he was going to
hit me in the back of the head or something but
he didn't. He was just cursing at me and trying to
make me feel low. But it didn't make a difference
any more.

"You bring that wine back up here," Lonnie
called down to me when I had got down the first
flight of steps. "And bring some cups, too."

I turned around and looked at him, standing
there in the doorway trying to be something. For
a minute I started to say how come he didn't
come on with me. But I knew he wasn't going to

come and I knew that I had to go. He was stuck in that place, maybe even standing right there in that doorway, being what he was. One thing I knew, though, was that I wasn't stuck there with him.

15

I walked slow over to Mr. Roland's house. The wind was blowing like it might rain soon and it made my face feel better. It was his day off and he was in bed, but he looked at me and asked me what the matter was, and I told him there was a guy in my house with a gun and another one who was shot up real bad. Mr. Roland's wife asked me if I was sure, and Mr. Roland said for her to look at how my face was swoll up if she didn't think I was sure. He started calling the police, and he asked me if there was anyone in the house beside the guy with the gun and the one who was dying. I told him there was another guy there, too.

When the police came they asked me some more questions and then we all went in two regular cars to where I lived. On the way I told them about the stickup and everything. I asked them if I had to go in with them and they said no, they would go in by themselves.

"The other guy in there, his name is Lonnie,"

I said. "He's my father. He don't have a gun or nothing."

"Don't worry, we won't hurt anybody," the cop said.

They went in and I prayed as hard as I could that they wouldn't hurt Lonnie. I don't know why I didn't want them to hurt him or why I felt bad about them going to get him, but I did.

The policeman that stayed in the car said I shouldn't worry, that mostly things worked out. He started talking about how he had a boy like me, but it wasn't true. He didn't have nobody like me because he wasn't like Lonnie.

It seemed like a long time, but after a while the police came downstairs with Lonnie and Stone and Denise. I don't know how Denise got up there, but they didn't have no handcuffs on her. She was crying, though, about Bubba, I guess.

What happened next was Lonnie and Stone went to jail and they let Denise go home. They sent a ambulance after Bubba. I had to go to a place where they sent boys who got into trouble and I hated it. I stayed in that place eight days and had about two fights every day while I was there. Then I had to go before a judge, and he told me about how much trouble I was in and things like that, and then he said that Mr. Roland had asked the court to have custody of me until things got settled. The judge asked me if I wanted to stay with Mr. Roland and I said okay. Then the judge started telling me how lucky I was to have somebody like him, meaning Mr. Roland, interested in me.

Mr. Roland took me home and told me he would help me all he could, and I asked him if he would please help Lonnie, because Lonnie was in big trouble. I thought I could do okay, better than a lot of people, and I wasn't in trouble because they dropped all the charges against me. Mr. Roland said that if he could do anything for Lonnie he would, only I think he was kind of disappointed that I asked.

Bubba died. He was in the hospital when he died, and everybody that knew him said how it was a shame. I thought Denise was really going to get messed up and everything, but she was okay. She asked me if I knew that Bubba had asked her to marry him and I said no, I didn't know that. She told me a lot about the wedding that they were going to have, and it was just like the practice wedding that me and her had.

Lonnie and Stone and Jackie had a trial and they said they were guilty. They wasn't charged with robbing the man, but with assault and having guns. It had something to do with the man who shot Bubba not having a permit for his gun, either. Anyway, Lonnie and Stone both got from three to five years, but the lawyer said that Lonnie would probably be out in a year and a half.

The jail they was sending Lonnie to was a long way away, and the judge said I could see Lonnie before he left.

It was like the rooms they had in the place where they kept me until Mr. Roland got me. There was a pool table in it and a Ping-Pong table. I was really kind of scared because I hadn't seen Lonnie or talked to him since he was arrested and went to jail. I thought he would probably hate me because of what I did. But I had got it sorted out in my mind. I didn't want Lonnie to hate me, I didn't want anybody to hate me, especially my father. But there was things I didn't want even more, like sneaking around hoping that the police wouldn't get me and only having friends like Stone and Bubba. Most of all I didn't want not to like myself any more, or do things so I wouldn't have to think about what I was doing. I was ready for Lonnie to hate me the same way I was ready for him to hit me on the night the cops came and took him away.

He came in with a guard and he walked over to me and raised his hand like he was going to give me five and I put my hand out and he gave me five.

"Hey, man, what's happening?" he said.

"I'm sorry," I said. I didn't want to look him in the face because I was really sorry that he was in jail.

"Hey, ain't nothing to it," he said. "That's just the way it goes. You did the right thing because that's just the way you are. I can dig it."

I looked up at him and his face was sad and he was trying to get up a smile, but it wasn't coming too easy. I figured he must have planned what he was going to say, but it still didn't make it easy.

"You okay?" I asked.

"Yeah," he answered. He sat down on a plastic couch they had in the room. "It ain't no soft bed but I'll hack it. Maybe get myself together. I don't know."

"The judge said maybe you can be out . . ." I started saying that the judge said he could get out in maybe a year and a half if he didn't get into no trouble, but it didn't really seem to matter.

We didn't say nothing for a while and then he asked me where I was going to be staying and I told him.

"You scared?" he asked.

"Scared?"

"About what's gonna happen."

"A little," I said. "But I think I'll get by. I'll be

okay, you know."

"You know that stuff I said about that guy?"

"Mr. Roland?"

"Yeah. Well, don't pay no mind to it," he said. "Sometime I get to talking and . . ."

"You think you going to be okay?"

"I guess so. You know, one time I told myself that I wasn't ever going to come back in this place no damn more. I was going to get out and get a good job and do all kinds of good shit. Damn! I don't even know what the hell happened." There was a magazine on the arm of the couch and it fell off and Lonnie picked it back up again. "Here I am, right back in this place. And you know what's funny?"

"What?"

"If they said, 'Hey, Lonnie, go on home. Right now.' I mean, if they let me right out of here right now, I wouldn't know if I'd be back in this place or not. Hey, look at me talking to you like this. I'm supposed to be telling you not to get into trouble, so you won't have to come here."

"Lonnie?"

"Yeah?"

"I ain't coming here. You don't have to tell me nothing because I ain't coming here."

"I guess you ain't," he said. He reached out his

hand like he was going to touch me or something, and then he pulled it back. "You going to write to me? I got to let everybody know I got me a big son out here on the street."

"Sure, I'll write."

"Take care of your grandma, too."

I nodded.

"This guy you staying with . . ." Whatever it was he was going to say he couldn't get it out. "Maybe when I get out of here we can get a little something going. I don't mean no father or son thing—it don't have to be nothing like that. Maybe we could just get together."

He looked up past me, and I turned and saw the guard pointing to his watch, and then Lonnie stood up and I stood up and he reached out and took my hand and we shook. It wasn't much, but it was all we could do.

"A father and son thing would be okay," I said.

Lonnie went to the door with the guard, and then he turned back and I could see his face was wet, and he gave me a little wave. Then the door closed, and he was gone.

I like Mr. Roland a lot but I'm kind of careful not to like him too much because I don't know what might happen. He buys me a lot of stuff but

I don't ask for nothing.

I write to Lonnie and he writes back to me. Sometimes I really look forward to getting his letters and I wonder why, because he hurt me more than anybody I know. I guess it's because he's my father and I want him and me to be okay, and maybe, when he gets out, we can get together like he said. And even if I feel, deep inside, that it really ain't going to be that way, I'm still hoping.